UNSELFISH DESIRES

notionpress.com

UNSELFISH DESIRES

Pravada Milind Telang

notionpress.com

Notion Press

Old No. 38, New No. 6
McNichols Road, Chetpet
Chennai - 600 031

First Published by Notion Press 2016

ISBN 978-81-7511-071-7

CONTENTS

Acknowledgement

First and foremost I would like to thank my husband who instilled the confidence in me to write. He has been my motivation. He has always given me the right inputs. My parents for inculcating the right values in me, especially my mother who always encouraged me all the times. My mother-in-law who taught me multitasking. My daughter who gave me valuable support in my writing, my son who kept on pushing me when I was down. My brother who always appreciated me. My aunts who were an integral part of my life and my dearest friends who were always with me in my ups and downs. The people who I would really like to thank from the bottom of my heart who helped me with book are Vishal Mergu, Mahesh Narale and last but not least Pooja Ranawat who were always there with me while writing my book and big thank you to the entire Notion Press team, that has guided me patiently through the publishing process.

FOREWORD

Unselfish desires is a book of women, by a woman but a must read for both men and women!

As much as women will find this book interesting, men will be able to understand psychology of women.

This book has almost read the psychology of a woman so well that when one reads the book, it appears you know the character of the story so well.

It is a compilation of short stories which one sees occurring in day to day lives of many of us. Dr. Pravada Telang, a Gynaecologist by profession who interacts with women closely through her profession, has captured lives of young women very well. These short stories are based on relationships between husband and wife, mother and daughter, aspirations of parents for their children, careless flings, ordeals of NRI parents, Psyche of infertile couples, etc.

In today's world with nuclear families, both partners working, ambitions and goals to be met with, couples do not have time to spend with each other or their children.

Work pressures and demanding careers of both men and women have led to relationships that are fragile and less trust worthy. With changing life styles and value systems, with emulating the west, with women constantly equating themselves with men with a feeing of .. 'Why should only boys have all the fun'. The fabric of 'typical Indian family' has broken.

With work pressures and ambitions to achieve higher and higher targets, Men give less time to their wives which sometimes may lead to such unselfish desires.

This book has really brought out the true image of a modern Indian woman.

An excellent compilation of short stories, unselfish desires is a book that will be a mirror to many young women.

I can only compare Dr. Pravada Telang with one of my favourite authors Sudha Murthy.

– Dr. Vidya Yeravdekar
Principal Director
Symbiosis

Expedition

Dhanshri waited impatiently for Raju to come back home. Raju had gone trekking to the Everest Base Camp. He was away for almost a fortnight. Every day Dhanshri prayed for his safe return. She never understood what joy her husband got by going through so much of trouble just for the sake of adventure.

Dhanshri, her mother-in-law and her two-year-old daughter were all looking forward to meet Rajendra or Raju as he was fondly called. Dhanshri's two-year-old daughter too sensed that there was some excitement in the family. Dhanshri said repeatedly "*Aaj Baba yenar, Aaj Baba yenar*." Finally, Raju arrived with a gang of five to six friends.

Anveya jumped towards Raju and she was with him. Raju's mother had tears in her eyes. Dhanshri welcomed Raju by performing a traditional "Arti" before he entered the house.

Raju's friend said "We should also go and climb the Everest, if we want our wives to welcome us with *rangolis* and *aartis*." Dhanshri felt awkward when Raju embraced her in front of everyone.

Dhanshri freed herself from Raju's arms and went to the kitchen to make tea and *bhajiyas* for all of them. Raju's friends said "Raju, take some rest now." However, Raju wanted to tell them his experience about the Everest Base Camp.

His friends said that they would come some other time listen to his "*Shorya Katha*."

Raju spoke as if he didn't hear them. "You have to experience the thrill of trekking in the Himalayas. I have no words to describe the journey to the base camp. The snow-covered mountains, the valleys, the Sherpas... Everything was just amazing. Dhanshri you must help me, I plan to make a short documentary on my trek."

"Aai, Dhani... throughout the journey back home, I have been thinking of only one thing. Next year I want to scale the Mount Everest." Aai and Dhanshri were both stunned to hear this. "Listen, I will definitely go next year but I will not go alone. I will take Dhanshri along." "*Kay tarich kay!*" his mother exclaimed. "Have you lost it Raju? I never stopped you from climbing mountains and now you want to take Dhanshri along. Don't forget that you have a two-year-old daughter and an old widowed mother who are all dependent on you."

"Aai please, please allow me to take Dhanshri. I would have taken you also Aai, but your asthma will not allow you to do anything." Raju's mother said, "Think about my old bones Raju. Dhanshri intervened their conversation. I feel breathless if I climb two flights of stairs. You are thinking of taking me to climb Mt. Everest! Have you seen how much weight I have put on after Anveya's birth."

Raju said "Don't worry we have ten months to prepare." His mother interrupted "Dhani come and help me lay the table. Dhanshri and I have taken a Iot of trouble to make today's dinner. It's not easy looking after a two-year-old daughter and cooking an elaborate menu."

"Raju go and have a bath. I will make hot *chapattis* for all of us." Dhanshri gave Raju his towel and change of clothes. "What luxury I am experiencing!" thought Raju. A hot bath in a clean bathroom was a luxury. Raju remembered the dingy bathrooms he had to use during the trek.

After a nice dinner, all of them went to sleep. After a long time, Dhanshri fell asleep. The man of the family brings a sense of security and completeness.

Raju felt good the next day. Dhanshri served him tea. She had made *idli* and *chutney* for breakfast. Raju asked her to switch on the fan and started reading the newspapers.

Raju was actually enjoying all the attention and love that was coming his way. "All this is because I was away for some time. Both Aai and Dhani have understood my importance" he thought.

His mother said "Raju, the school is going to reopen on Monday. The rains will start. There is nothing in the house. Dhanshri and you should go and get groceries for the month." Raju promised to do the needful in the evening.

"Dhanshri... how much do you weigh now? You need to lose weight and Dhani you eat without thinking."

Dhanshri asked "Raju are you serious about your Mt. Everest expedition?" Raju responded "Of course darling I am serious." Dhanshri was not used to these kind of words from Raju. His way of expressing love was saying "*Murkh*," (stupid) or "*Gadav*" (asshole). "Dhani you are my legally wedded wife and I want you to accompany me when I scale the Everest. Mr and Mrs Jagtap the first couple from Maharashtra to climb the Everest. Raju held Dhanshri's hand and started dancing. Raju's mother entered the room. "I think one of the ghosts from the mountains has haunted your husband." Dhanshri responded "He is your son first and then my husband." Both Dhanshri and Aai burst out laughing. Raju looked at both of them and said "Say whatever you want but I will do what I have decided."

The same evening Raju and Dhanshri left home to purchase groceries. Raju did not allow Dhani to buy the usual quota of rice. He added a lot of pulses to the grocery list. Raju made Dhani buy green tea. Dhanshri said "I cannot live without rice." Raju responded "That's why you look like a gunny bag filled with rice." Dhanshri felt very bad.

"Let's go and buy a tracksuit for you" Raju said. Dhanshri pleaded "Please don't do this. We have already spent a lot on the groceries. We have to pay my mobile bill too. Do you remember how many times I called on your *thupka*?"

Dhanshri's parents had come to meet Raju. Raju's mother had already briefed them about Raju's plan. She had requested Dhanshri's father to talk to Raju.

Dhanshri's father said "You have lost a lot of weight Rajendra! And you are looking absolutely tired. You look older than your age." Raju responded testily "Do I have to enter the Mr Universe competition to look good and smart?" Dhanshri's father was taken aback on hearing Raju's answer.

He persisted, "Rajendra, Dhanshri is my only daughter. She was born after her mother had two boys. She is the youngest and the most pampered child in the family. I will not allow you to take her on some trekking expedition to Mount Everest! We have only seen pictures of the tallest mountains and that also in our geography books. We are simple folks from middle class families. Such adventures don't suit us."

He continued, "Don't forget you have an old mother and a two-year-old girl." Raju said "I understand my responsibilities. Why don't you understand I want my wife to be a part of this mission, I want to create history? Instead of encouraging us, all of you are pulling us back. Dhanshri, do you want to accompany me? You have the right to say no if you feel so." Dhanshri didn't expect a scene like this. "I will do whatever you say. Raju, I don't think I have the fitness or the courage to do so. I know my limitations." Raju said "Now that you have said yes, it is my duty to train you. Mrs Dhanshri Jagtap, your training starts from tomorrow." Dhanshri parents left Dhanshri's house without even saying bye to them. Raju looked at his mother and said "Aai, these people are with blinkers. They cannot think anything out of the box. I know you are not like them. I am confident that you will support Dhanshri and me in our endeavors. We need your blessings and help."

School began as usual. The first day at school coincided with the SSC results. The same year the school got very good results. A student from their school scored the highest marks in Maths, which happened to be the subject Raju taught. Rajendra was very elated. The management felicitated Rajendra Jagtap for hundred percent result in Maths. The principal also mentioned about Rajendra sir's expedition to Everest Base Camp. Rajendra was all smiles and happy. Dhanshri too was very happy with Rajendra's accomplishments.

"This man will give one hundred percent to everything he does," thought Dhanshri. After assembly, all students gathered around Rajendra sir to listen to his talk on the expedition to the Everest.

Rajendra promised all of them that he would share his experience with them after school.

All teachers gathered in the staff room. Everyone was asking him about his Everest Base Camp trek. "You are really very bold Rajendra. You need a lot of courage to do things like this. Look at me!" said Mr Gaikwad, the science teacher. "Twenty-five years of service, I still have to go to Goa. Well done Rajendra!"

Raju said "I want to tell you all something. I am planning to scale Mount Everest next year. This time I will not go alone. I intend to take my wife Dhanshri along with me." Everyone was shocked to hear this. "Rajendra we understand you are a daredevil but did you consider if Dhanshri will be able to undergo the hardships."

Mrs Phadke who was the oldest teacher in school went up to Dhanshri. "Dhanshri you should consider yourself lucky. Your husband wishes that you must accompany him on this expedition. It is very rare for a husband to think so much about his wife. You should be a part of this adventurous feat. Give it your best. God blesses all those who work hard to achieve their goals. Look at me this year. I will be retiring. I have not done anything besides teaching and looking after my children and now my grandchildren. Only the select few get to do something like this."

Dhanshri was moved by Mrs Phadke's words.

After school, Raju and Dhanshri went home as usual. Dhanshri started doing her household chores. Raju said "Dhanshri I need to talk to you, look we have to plan everything now. First and foremost, you will start getting up early. We will start jogging from tomorrow. When we come back from school, we will do yoga and some stretching exercises. Remember you have to be physically fit and mentally strong."

Dhanshri said "Raju, I need to spend time with Anveya as well." Raju responded "Dhanshri you have to steal time now. Bacchindri Pal should be your inspiration now." Dhanshri never thought that she would be doing something like Bacchindri Pal. She taught her students the lesson about her courage. "There is something known as multitasking. Dhanshri I have seen the Sherpa women. They manage their homes, they act as tourist guides.

You will be surprised! They even work as coolies." Raju showed Dhanshri a snap of a Nepali woman carrying a baby on her back and serving food at a tea house.

Raju had set the alarm for 4 am the next morning. Dhanshri got up with a start. She made tea for both of them. Dhanshri carried Anveya and made her sleep next to her mother-in-law.

Raju said "First few days you walk and then you jog." Raju was walking very fast. Dhanshri found it difficult to keep up with him. She said "I am feeling breathless." Raju said "Dhanshri, rest for some time. Take long deep breaths. When you begin exercising for the first time, it takes some time for your body to adjust to the physical exertion. Once you get used to this regime, you won't feel like this. I have planned everything meticulously for you. The first month, we only walk and jog. You should be able to do so without feeling tired. We concentrate on improving your stamina. The second month, we include cycling. The third month, we start climbing up and down Parvati hill. The fourth month, we start climbing Sinhagad. The fifth month, we start doing rope climbing. Every weekend we will go for trekking on the nearby hills." Dhanshri was sweating profusely. It was ages since she had done any exercises.

After coming home, Raju ran to take a shower. Where does he get the energy from? Dhanshri made tea. Dhanshri found it difficult even to walk till the kitchen platform. Her mother-in-law signaled her to rest for some time. "You have to attend school."

Dhanshri could feel every bone in her body aching. "This is called sweet pain" said Raju. She responded "Sweet pain! I never knew you could call pain sweet." Raju said "This Sunday we have to attend a seminar on Mt. Everest expedition." Dhanshri said "Oh God! My mother has called me to stay at her place. What will I tell her?" Raju sensed that Dhanshri was preoccupied with her thoughts. "My mother has…" before Dhanshri could complete her sentence, Raju shook her.

He said sternly "Rise above these petty issues. We are going on a difficult mission."

Within a week, there was a lot of difference in Dhanshri. Raju too was very surprised with the change in Dhanshri.

On Sunday, Raju and Dhanshri entered the auditorium. There were lovely posters of the snow clad mountains. There were two Nepali men on the dias. They belonged to the Sagarmatha Mountaineering Institute of Kathmandu. This institute would train people and organize treks. These two Sherpas were official guides and they would accompany mountaineers on the trekking expeditions. The two Sherpas were traveling all over the world to motivate people to take up mountaineering. One of them had scaled the Everest twice. They gave them the details of the permissions to be taken from the government of Nepal. When they told them of the expenses, Dhanshri felt the ground slipping below her feet. She nudged Raju. He signaled her to shut up and concentrate on what the Nepali guides were explaining. They showed them the route that they were to take.

Dhanshri developed goose bumps while seeing the base camp, i.e., Everest Base Camp route on the map.

The Sherpas spoke about their experiences for the past forteen years. One of them belonged to the family of Sherpa Tenzing who accompanied Edmund Hillary. The foreigners had a lot of costly trekking gear and equipment. The Indians fared very well due to their sheer determination. Next year the Mount Everest expedition was scheduled to begin on March 29th. If everything went smoothly without any interruptions, it would end on May 30th.

"You don't worry about the expenses. I have decided to sell the land we own in our village. After all it was left for me. What is the use of having money in a bank? Let's utilize our money for our goals." Raju had to run pillar to post to organize the funds. The teachers understood how much funds were required. The staff too contributed for Raju's expedition. Dhanshri's mother handed over her jewelry to them. Both Dhanshri and Raju were moved by this gesture.

Raju and Dhanshri summarized their routes mentally. Dhanshri worked hard for her fitness. Raju took her to a physician. He carried out all the tests that were required. Raju was a little scared. In his mind, he worried whether Dhanshri would acclimatize to the heights.

Dhanshri ate, slept and dreamt only about the expedition. After a few months of training, Dhanshri looked like an athlete. She looked much younger and fitter.

Eight months just flew by. Raju had carried out all the technical formalities that were required for the expedition. Finally, the day of departure arrived. Dhanshri was a bag of mixed emotions. Her Aai and Baba came to see her off. Anveya was too young to understand anything.

Her mother and mother-in-law assured her that they would take care of Anveya. Raju's mother performed a puja for their safe return. All their neighbors and teachers from their school came to see them off.

The train left for Mumbai. They had to catch a flight to Kathmandu. "Raju, I am feeling scared, will I be able to keep up to your expectations? Don't worry, be positive and be confident." Raju put his arms around her. It was the first time Dhanshri was traveling out of India. "Let's enjoy our first international travel." It was a two-hour flight. A volunteer from the trekking institute was standing with a placard to welcome them. Kathmandu was a nice place. The volunteer's name was Dhansingh. Dhansingh told them about tourism in Nepal. "When you come back you must stay for a day or two and see Kathmandu" he said.

Their rooms were booked at the Himalaya Institute of Trekking. The maid who was making their room ready asked them their names. She looked at Dhanshri and said women go up to the Everest Base Camp, they rarely climb Mt. Everest. "Anyways there are exceptions to the rules. Stay back and relax today. Have a nice bath before you start. You may not get clean bathrooms in the tea houses." Dhanshri had not thought about this. "How am I going to manage?" she thought. The same evening they interacted with many people who were going to the Everest Base Camp. They met many people who were coming back from the base camp. Some were happy and some were unhappy. Some had to return midway due to mountain sickness.

Dhanshri and Rajendra were introduced to Sherpa Gyanendra and Sherpa Laxman. They were to accompany them. Sherpa Gyanendra was a "Sirdar," that is, an experienced Sherpa. He had scaled the Everest before Sherpa Laxman was known as Lucky. He was a young fellow and was going on the Everest expedition for the first time. Dhanshri felt very comfortable with them. Sherpa Gyanendra cheered Dhanshri. He said a lot of people go to the base camp, but very few dared to climb. He asked her if she minded him calling her "Dhannoo."

The next day they look a flight to Lukla. Their trekking would begin from Lukla. Gyaniji advised all of them to take a tablet of diamox every day. "It helps in acclimatization," he said. He had a stock of emergency medicines with him. When they arrived at Lukla, Gyaniji and Lucky asked them to worship a local goddess before beginning their expedition. Dhanshri too had an idol of Lord Ganapati in her backpack.

They began their expedition at 7 am sharp. They walked continuously. Dhanshri and Lucky would continuously talk to each other. Gyaniji advised both of them not to talk much. He asked them to concentrate on their trek. "We have miles to go, don't waste your energy talking."

They would wait for a few minutes in between. They walked till 3 pm. Gyaniji said they would rest at a tea tree house. Just as they approached the tree house, they heard a lot of hustle and bustle. They had reached Namche Bazar. There were lots of people in Namche Bazar. You could hear a lot of people talking on their thupkas. Thupkas were satellite phones used by mountaineers. Dhanshri and Rajendra spoke to their parents at home. Little Anveya was overjoyed to hear her mother's voice. They could hear Hindi movie songs. The local tea house was playing these songs. "Look how popular Hindi music has become" said Dhanshri.

Dhanshri made tea from Girnar tea sachets they were carrying. The tea was very refreshing. Tengboche was their next destination.

Raju started complaining of headache the next day. They had to stop their trek before the schedule. "He will settle down, don't worry" said Gyaniji. He asked Rajendra to take a painkiller and sleep. There were a lot of Nepali and Tibetan women at Tengboche. Dhanshri was surprised that most of them spoke Hindi and English. There were masseurs who massaged the feet of the climbers. Dhanshri felt very uncomfortable when the Tibetan woman massaged her feet. The Tibetan lady explained that her massage would improve the blood flow in her feet. Their next destination was Lobuche.

After a good night sleep, all four were ready for their trek the next day. Their trek till the Everest Base Camp was very uneventful. "Tomorrow our real journey starts" said Gyaniji. "I am very impressed with Dhanoo" said Gyaniji. I thought she will say let's go back. "No, No, Gyaniji our aim is to reach Sagarmatha." Gyaniji asked them to call home. He said that there might not be coverage. Over their satellite phones, she heard her daughter blabber on the phone. "My baby is millions of miles away." Dhanshri broke down crying. Raju too felt a lump in his throat. He said "C'mon Dhanshri cheer up. We have completed half of our mission."

Just then, they heard a huge crash. An avalanche had come down from Pumori. Dhanshri was very scared. The avalanche was only a few meters away from them.

The next morning they began their trek towards icefall, which was about 6100 meters above the sea level. There were boulders of ice that would just give away. All four of them trekked very steadily and slowly. They regularly stopped for their soup and tea breaks. Instant tea and soup were their life savers. Gyaniji and Lucky set up a tent for them to spend the night. The place was absolutely stunning. Rajendra captured many pictures in his camera.

Gyaniji and Lucky sang songs at all times. All four of them played Antakshari. This was their only stress buster.

From here, they got a first glimpse of the Everest.

"Our main test starts when we reach camp III or Lhotse wall." To boost their confidence, Gyaniji said "camp IV and then we will reach the summit." Dhanshri too was elated. She could not believe that they were just a little distance away from their destination. All of them concentrated on their climb. Dhanshri constantly chanted the Hanuman Chalisa. She believed that it was the power above that gave them the strength to carry on their expedition. "Let's wait here for some time" said Gyaniji. Just then, they heard some groans. The groans echoed due to the silence. Gyaniji signaled everyone to stay quiet so that that they could locate the place where the sounds came from. "You all wait here I will go and see" said Lucky. "No. Let's all go together" said Rajendra. After walking a few steps ahead, they saw a person lying buried under a heap of snow. They did not know for how long he had been lying there. His breathing was also very shallow. All four of them removed him from the heap of ice. Lucky put his oxygen mask on his face. His toes had turned absolutely black due to frost bite.

Lucky and Gyaniji massaged his body to improve the blood flow. Lucky, Rajendra and Gyaniji tried calling the base camp to ask them for help. Their satellite phones were not working. It was a very tricky situation. All four of them used their knowledge of resuscitation to make this person breathe. What do we do now?

"Saheb, if we leave him like this he will die here, his body will get buried in the ice." Dhanshri said "How can we do this to him? All of us should go down with him." Gyaniji, Lucky and Rajendra were all surprised with Dhanshri's decision. "See if we take him down we will be able to get aid for him and at least we can try to save his life." Gyaniji, Lucky and Rajendra were not in favor of going back. They said "See his companions have left him. Why should we ruin our expedition?" "Are our personal aspirations and goals more important than someone's life," said Dhanshri.

Gyaniji said "Look Sir and Madam, we are here to accompany you. Whatever decision you take we will follow." Lucky was feeling very bad. Gyaniji signaled him not to give his opinion.

Dhanshri said "It's our duty to try and help him. We don't know his details." Lucky managed to find his backpack. This person was from Germany. His name was Phil Maino. "Forget everything, he is a human being and we can save his life. His foot will need amputation. He can live with one foot. Let's go back." Lucky and Gyaniji made a stretcher from their tents. Rajendra was very upset. "Look Dhanshri, look at the Everest. We are so near, but.... Dhanshri. Thank you for making me realize what humanity is." Dhanshri too was very sad. So were Gyaniji and Lucky, but without letting their emotions overwhelm them. All four of them started climbing down. Dhanshri's eyes were filled with tears. She was thinking about Rajendra's dream and the efforts she had put to attain the fitness. Everything had a taken a back seat now. Their only aim was to save Phil. They started walking towards the base camp.

CELEBRATION

"Ma don't forget to bring my sparklers and paper plates while coming home." Arundhati's daughter had called her to remind her of the things she wanted for craft the next day in school. "Aditi how many times I have warned you to tell me what you want in advance. When are you going to change? This is the last time I am warning you. Next time you ask for something at the eleventh hour, I am not going to get anything for you." "These children are so troublesome" she murmured so herself. Aditi called again. "Ma, Ma I forgot to tell you that Parobai is not coming." Her mother said, "Aditi, couldn't you tell me this before?"

Arundhati said, "Today only I decided to stay overtime to finish of the pending loan proposals."

Arundhati quickly logged out. She had to do it carefully. She remembered the last time there was a frantic call from home. She had pressed the delete button and all her files had got deleted.

Arundhati left her cabin in a hurry. She requested the peon to switch off the lights in her cabin.

Why am I so dependent on Parobai? I have told her so many times. She is supposed to call me on my mobile, but no she has understood that I can't do without her. I must find a replacement for her that will teach her a lesson.

When she reached her car, she saw the peon rushing towards her, "Madam you forgot your tiffin bag in the office." Arundhati thought of calling her husband to ask him to buy the list of things Aditi wanted. "It's useless telling him to do anything. He will blame me for not disciplining the children."

Poor Arundhati reached home with Aditi's sparklers and paper plates. "Ma, I am feeling very hungry." Arundhati rushed to the kitchen and did not have time to change her clothes. She quickly made cheese toast for Aditi.

Aditi agreed to eat what Arundhati had made and did not argue. At times, Arundhati felt she was too strict with the kids. "Where is your brother?" "He has not come back from his Maths tuitions" said Aditi. Arundhati asked "Why is he so late?" Aditi replied "Ma he has a test tomorrow. So he said he will come back late."

Arundhati changed quickly into a cotton *salwar kameez*. She opened the fridge to see what was there... She saw cluster beans. She thought "Oh no! Sameer will blow his top, if I make cluster beans in the evening for dinner." Arundhati remembered that she had shelled green peas. I will make "*aloo mutter*." It's easier to decide the E.M.I.S. terms and conditions for home loans than to decide what to make for dinner. She washed the dal and rice and put them in the cooker. The aroma of the *aloo mutter* filled the house.

Arundhati realized Parobai's worth in her absence. It's my fault also. I should have called home as usual to find out what the kids were doing. My Ajinkya would have told me Parobai is not coming.

Arundhati's cell rang. Aditi why don't you pick up the phone. "Ma, it's your phone." "Aditi, I know it's my phone. Can't you pick it up? You know I am cooking." Aditi said "Ma, before I could answer, it got cut off." Arundhati said "at least see who was calling." Aditi said "Ma, it's an unknown number."

Aditi placed the cell phone on the kitchen platform. Arundhati said "Very smart Aditi, so that you can watch your Pokemon undisturbed."

Arundhati's phone rang again. She answered the phone while making the *chapatties*. "Mrs Arundhati Sarnaik, congratulations, I am calling on behalf of Sakal Papers. Mr Gautam Joshi here. You are one of the nominees of 'Pune Achievers Awards.' You have bagged this prestigious award for your remarkable contribution in the field of housing finance. In the past three years, you have made everyone's dream of owning a house achievable."

Arundhati couldn't believe this was happening to her. For a moment she felt as though the world had come to a halt. Arundhati had launched a website that gave details of how to procure home loans. She had written a book on how to go and buy a new house. Her company helped people procure home loans. They would help people right from buying homes till they shifted into their new homes. The entire project "Dream Homes" was Arundhati's idea.

"Aditi, Aditi come here Baccha." Aditi was too young to understand Arundhati's achievement. Just then, Ajinkya entered. He was elder to Aditi. He understood his mother's achievement. "Ma does Pappa know about this." "No beta I just received the phone call from Sakal Papers." Sameer was overjoyed when he heard the news. "I will reach in half an hour's time and then we shall celebrate." Just then, Ma Saheb, Arundhati's mother-in-law, entered the house and Ajinkya broke the news to her. "Wow! Arundhati, well done," this was the first time her mother-in-law was praising her. Arundhati bent down to touch her feet to seek her blessings.

Ma Saheb said "Arundhati remember I was instrumental in pushing you to do MBA. Remember I not only financed your MBA but I also looked after Ajinkya while you were studying."

Arundhati remembered the difficulties she faced while doing her MBA. Ma Saheb asked "Arundhati, what have you made for dinner? Parobai has not come." This means she knew that Parobai was not coming. "The older she is getting, the meaner she is being," Arundhati mumbled to herself.

"Couldn't she stay at home for one evening? I wonder what she learns in the 'Gita Discourse' that she attends every evening. Behave properly with your daughter-in-law and that's the easiest way of achieving Moksha."

Arundhati didn't want to spoil her happiness. At least not today. She said "Come, I will serve food to the three of you."

Arundhati laid the table and served them food. "Arundhati you should have added tomato puree to the *subji*. It makes it nice and thick." Arundhati mumbled to herself "Can't this lady eat without grumbling?" Ajinkya noted the tension in the air. "Ma your *subji* today is exactly like they make in hotels."

Sameer congratulated Mrs Sarnaik "Chalo, Chalo Party," he said. "Arundhati, why did you serve food to the children? We could have gone out." Ajinkya had a Maths test the next day and Aditi was feeling sleepy.

Sameer said "At least order something sweet." Ajinkya ran to the phone "I will order butterscotch ice cream." The grocer would deliver it as he did home delivery till eleven in the night. "Aru let's go out for dinner, the children will sleep." Arundhati refused to go out for dinner with Sameer. "I have taken a lot of trouble in making dinner today. Parobai took chutti without informing me." Sameer said "Who asked you to cook? We could have gone out for dinner." Arundhati was very annoyed with Sameer's remarks.

"Thankless" she said. Sameer said "Did you say something?" Arundhati said "I was asking if we can have dinner now. Serve me dinner in the hall. Sameer don't create a mess on the sofa." As usual Sameer was channel surfing. He saw Arundhati's photo flash on one of the channels. "Arundhati come here quickly." Sam TV Marathi was showing "The achievers of Pune awardees." Ma Saheb, Arundhati and the children all rushed towards the hall.

The newsreader was talking about the Young Achiever's list of the year that was nominated by Sakal Papers. Arundhati's phone was ringing continuously for the next one hour. This was something she had never imagined. Arundhati thanked everyone for their wishes.

It was quarter to twelve. Arundhati was very tired. She set the alarm for quarter to six and changed. Arundhati realized that Sameer was watching her change. "Arundhati you have put on so much of weight in the wrong places. You have tyres on your stomach. Remember how you were a few years back."

Arundhati said irritatedly "Sameer I was not a mother of two then and I am not a model to have a flat stomach." Sameer said "For me you are a super model Arundhati." Sameer tried to pull her close. Arundhati pushed him away. "First you criticize, then you call me a super model. Sameer have you ever thought how I rush from morning to night." Sameer said "Oh! Aru don't begin again." Just then, the phone rang. Sameer answered the phone most unwillingly. "It's for you Aru." Arundhati exclaimed "For me! Who is it at this hour?" Arundhati tried to balance herself and she reached for the receiver. "Were you sleeping beta? You must be tired." After she heard her mother's voice, she had a lump in her throat. "I told your Appa we will call her tomorrow morning but he just wouldn't listen." Her father then spoke "Abhinandan, Aru you have made your old father very proud today." Arundhati felt she would burst out crying after she heard her father's voice. Sameer had pulled a pillow across his face to avoid listening to their conversation.

The alarm on her cell phone started beeping. Arundhati jumped out of bed. “Ajinkya has a test today; I should have woken him up early.”

Arundhati reached the kitchen to make tea for Sameer with toothbrush still in her mouth. Ma Saheb gave her an irritated look. “Arundhati brush your teeth and then enter the kitchen.” Arundhati couldn’t retort with the tooth brush in her mouth.

Sameer had his tea and left for the race course for his morning walk. Arundhati went to the children’s bedroom. Ajinkya was at his study table solving algebra equations. “Why didn’t you tell me you were awake Baccha?” Just then, Aditi got up in her bed and started crying. Arundhati held her close and asked her why she was crying. “Lost my new Barbie watch yesterday. Doesn’t matter, don’t cry. I will buy you another one.”

Ajinkya shouted from his study table “Ma don’t buy anything for her, she lost her pen last week.” Aditi ran towards Ajinkya to pull his hair. Ajinkya retaliated by pushing her hard. Arundhati tried to separate them. Aditi screamed at the top of her voice. Ma Saheb entered listening to their shouts.

“Ajinkya go back to your study table at once. Arundhati, they behave like this only when they see you.” Arundhati made the children eat breakfast. Arundhati was tying Aditi’s plaits and she could not find her school ribbons. “How many times have I told you to keep your things safe.” Poor Arundhati rummaged the entire dressing table. She remembered she had kept a roll of ribbons in her cupboard for emergency.

Finally, the children got ready and left for school. What a relief! Ma Saheb was reading the newspaper loudly.

The news of Arundhati's award was in the newspaper. Arundhati saw Ma Saheb swell with pride. Ma Saheb was calling all her relatives to tell them about Arundhati's achievement.

Arundhati couldn't believe that it was the same Ma Saheb who was calling people to tell them about Arundhati's award.

Ma Saheb always criticized Arundhati. "Arundhati has mediocre dreams," she would say. Arundhati had learnt over the years to ignore her. In a way, her criticism proved to be a blessing in disguise. These remarks made Arundhati set higher goals for herself. Arundhati had a cup of tea and ran to her bedroom to get ready for office. Arundhati went to the cupboard to see what to wear that day. She chose a blue chiffon saree. She found a string of pearls to match with the saree.

Arundhati believed in the term power dressing. One has to be well dressed to form a good impression. Arundhati's cabin was filled with congratulatory notes and flowers.

Sameer had organized a surprise party for all their friends and Arundhati's office colleagues in "Blue Diamond." Arundhati was overwhelmed by his gesture. Sameer had ordered a multicuisine dinner for at least seventy to eighty guests.

Arundhati's Aai had called her home for dinner that night. Arundhati was in a dilemma. She didn't have the courage to tell Sameer that her parents had called them for dinner. She did not have the guts to break her old mother's heart.

Arundhati stayed till about 9 pm at Sameer's party. She left the party under the pretense of a splitting headache. She caught an auto to reach Navi Peth where her parents lived. Her mother was standing in the balcony waiting for her. Arundhati realized that her parents were staying in the same house for over forty years now. The building was very old and it did not have a lift. Arundhati murmured to herself. "Arundhati Sarnaik, the super achiever. You fulfill everyone's dreams of owning their houses. What about your Anna and Aai? Still in the same old house." Just then, Aai opened the door. The house was filled with the aroma of *Puran Poli and Katachi Amti*. "Aru where is Sameer? Why have you came alone? Can we ever celebrate your success without Sameer?"

Trapped

Tanvi was getting ready to go out for dinner. She was wearing a long skirt and a blouse over it. Tanvi had tied her hair into a high pony tail. She was applying *kohl* over her eyes, when Somu entered. Somu looked at her and asked her to wear a *stole* around her neck. "You will look better." Tanvi caught hold of Somu teasingly and asked him from where he got the idea.

Somu pushed her aside and started looking at himself in the mirror. "I have a better dressing sense than you. I have a good choice." Tanvi laughed "Yeah! You have a good choice. I agree with you Somshekhar Aiyyar."

Somshekhar Aiyyar wanted to fling his comb at Tanvi. But Tanvi caught hold of him. Their so-called skirmish ended with a tight hug and passionate kissing. Tanvi tried to relieve herself from Somu's clutches. "Dear husband please stop, there is no dinner. I have no intention of cooking anything now. Let's get out and have dinner first."

Somu said "How can you be so boring Tanvi? You are thinking of dinner when I am holding you love." Tanvi said "Somu, I have not had anything, I am famished. Let's get going." "*Pehle Vithoba Mag Potoba. Yeh kya hai? Tanvi yaar Tumhari Marathi mat Zhado! yaar.*"

"Somu you are married to a Marathi Mulgi so you need to listen to my Marathi dialogs. Somu do I complain when you listen to your Tamil songs." Somu said "That's because they are melodious." Tanvi said "Chalo Mr Tamil let's lock our house and get going. Let's have Chinese today." Somu took Tanvi to the Chinese room. After dinner, both of them walked hand in hand like old times.

Somu and Tanvi were married for almost a year now. Both of them worked in a multinational company.

Tanvi was a linguistic expert. She spoke German and French fluently. Tanvi and Somu met during a seminar held in his company. Tanvi trained executives to speak in German. Somu was very impressed with Tanvi. He found her extremely attractive and smart. For Somshekhar Aiyyar, it was love at first sight. Somu succeeded in wooing Tanvi.

There was a lot of opposition from Somu's side. Somu's mother was totally shattered when she heard her boy's decision of marrying a Maharashtrian girl. Somu's father was more liberal than his mother. He expressed his desire to meet Tanvi.

Somu's father came all the way to Pune from Chennai. He liked Tanvi a lot. "We have no daughter Tanvi, two boys. I am happy to welcome you as a daughter that I missed." Tanvi, found his father very affectionate. She developed a liking for him. At once, Appa told Tanvi about Amma. "Amma is like a coconut, hard to crack, but she is very affectionate. My wife is a teacher so she is a little strict." Tanvi was nervous when she heard this. Tanvi's parents were also disturbed when Tanvi told them about Somu.

"Tanvi you cannot live without eating nonvegetarian food. How will you adjust in a south Indian family?" Tanvi said "Aai I taught Somu to eat nonveg now. He has no hassles about my eating habits." They said "It's ok with your husband, but think about your 'Sasubai'."

"*AyyoTanvi kyakhata tum.*" Aai teased Tanvi. "Aai don't worry they are in Chennai, we are here in Pune. How does it matter?" They were not satisfied. "Look Tanvi as your parents we are trying to tell you the difficulties." Tanvi said "As long as Somu is there, I don't care."

"This girl has gone crazy. I am telling you she thinks it's easy. These girls, they are financially independent, they think it's easy. I had difficulties in adjusting to my in-laws Tanvi." "Aai stop it, your times were different" said Tanvi.

There were a lot of differences among the two families regarding the marriage ceremony. Finally, Somu and Tanvi settled for a court marriage. Tanvi had always dreamt about a grand wedding, but her dreams about the marriage ceremony were shattered.

Somu and Tanvi went to Chennai after their wedding. Tanvi found her mother-in-law to be very charming. She wore diamonds in her ears and nose. Somu lived in a palatial bungalow.

Tanvi had to get her nose pierced at her mother-in-law's insistence. Amma presented Tanvi with diamonds just like the ones she wore. Tanvi didn't understand a word of their conversations. Somu acted as an interpreter.

Appa and Amma took them around all the temples. Tanvi conversed with her in-laws either in English or in Hindi.

Tanvi's brief stay with her in-laws came to an end on a very affectionate note. Tanvi was very excited when they returned back to Pune. Somu had brought a new place for them. Tanvi was overjoyed to move into her new house. "Finally my house, I am the queen of this place." At home, when she wanted to do something her mother always found some fault in her decision. If Aai liked it, Dada her father didn't like it. If her parents liked it, her brother and Vahini didn't like it. "Redo your house as you want Tanvi when you get married" they once said.

So finally, Tanvi had her own house. Tanvi had many ideas as to how to do the house. "A major part of my salary will be deducted for the home loan so be a little slow," Somu warned Tanvi.

Tanvi assured Somu that she had saved a lot of money in the last three years. "Somu, please let me do the house as per my choice, I won't touch your bank balance."

Tanvi went a little overboard but the final result was amazing. Tanvi had done her house very tastefully.

Tanvi had taken great pains in choosing everything. The curtains and the sofas were her choice. Tanvi meticulously chose every little thing. She purchased a lot of indoor plants. Tanvi went around the whole of Pune gathering artifacts.

Tanvi was overjoyed to do things without interference. Somu didn't give her any inputs for the house. He realized that Tanvi was obsessed about their home décor. So he chose to stay away. Days and weeks just flew away. Somu was a no nonsense person. He rarely interfered in Tanvi's day-to-day activities. Every night, he spoke to his Amma and Appa in Tamil.

"Somu I am going to learn Tamil now. Then I will come to know what you talk to your Amma and Appa."

Amma and Appa talked to Tanvi as well, but their conversation remained the same.

"Ponnu," that's what Appa called her. Somu told her Ponnu meant daughter in Tamil. "*Ponu Khana Khaya?* Take care of your health. Is Somu troubling you?"

Sometimes to break the monotony of the conversation, Tanvi asked Appa how he spent his day.

Tanvi noticed that Somu was restless for the past two days. Tanvi asked him the reason for his restlessness. "Tanvi, Amma is retiring next week. Appa and Amma have always worked so hard. Can I call them to spend sometime with us?"

"Somshekhar Aiyyar, do you require my permission to call your parents? Go ahead and call them. It will be great to have them here." Tanvi wanted to show her in-laws how tastefully she had done their house.

Somu called up Amma and Appa and asked them to come to Pune. Both of them agreed at once. Somu sent them air tickets. Somu was very excited as his folks were going to stay with them for the first time. He said "Tanvi. We will take them to Dagadusheth Ganpati. Tanvi try and come early when they are here."

She said "Ok! Ok as you say dear!" Finally, the day Appa and Amma were to come dawned.

Somu went alone to pick them up. Tanvi stayed at home. She wanted to make breakfast for them. They had caught an early morning flight.

As soon as Amma came, she threw her purse on the mat. She lay down on the sofa. "I am feeling sick I don't like this air travel. Somu next time, I will come by train. Tanvi please make some coffee dear." Tanvi made coffee and served it in glass mugs. "Ayyo! Tanvi I can't drink coffee in a glass mug." Tanvi gave Somu an angry glance. Stupid fellow had not told me anything about Amma's choices. How could I forget I had seen her drinking coffee in a stainless steel glass in Chennai? Appa made no fuss at all. He sipped his coffee quietly.

Tanvi showed them their room. Tanvi carried their bags to their room.

"Nice house. Very well done," said Appa. "It must have cost a fortune," Amma interrupted him.

Tanvi said "Appa and Amma you rest now. I have to go to office. I have an induction program." Amma said "Somu said he would stay at home." Tanvi found this strange. He had not told her about his leave today. Whenever Tanvi pleaded him to take an occasional leave, he gave many reasons and said no. Tanvi gave instructions to the maid and left. The same evening, when Tanvi returned from office, her house was completely changed. All the bonsai plants from the hall had vanished. She asked Somu about her plants. Amma has shifted them to the terrace.

Her sofa and cozy settee had exchanged places. Amma and Appa can't sit up for a long time. So I exchanged positions so that they can lie down and watch TV.

Amma made strong filter coffee and served it to Tanvi in a stainless steel glass. Tanvi smiled as she sipped the coffee. Somu was all smiles today. He started praising the *rasam* Amma had made for lunch. Somu asked Tanvi to taste it. Tanvi gave a perplexed look "*Rasam and Bhaat* at this hour! I will have it for dinner."

Tanvi went to the kitchen to place the empty coffee glasses. Tanvi felt she was entering someone else's kitchen. Tanvi's cooking ware was replaced with a new set of steel utensils. On God! Just one day, this lady has changed everything. I feel like a stranger in my own house. Tanvi went to her room to change. As usual she wore her cotton pyjamas and T-shirt. Amma gave Tanvi such a stern look that Tanvi ran to her room to change. She changed again into a salwar kameez. Amma reminded her to wear a *bindi* on her forehead. Somu was a silent spectator to all this. Tanvi stamped Somu's foot angrily. Amma asked Tanvi to get ready. She wanted to go shopping. Tanvi was very tired. She had a very hectic day at office. But Tanvi couldn't say no to her. Amma purchased a lot of grocery items, Tanvi had not even heard the names of some of things she got. Amma brought all the vegetables that Somu liked, She didn't even bother to ask about Tanvi's preferences. Even after shopping so much, Amma had the energy to make payasam for Somu.

The next day Amma and Appa were awake at 5 am. Tanvi got up with a start at 6:00 am. Tanvi felt as if she had done a crime. Tanvi asked Amma what she should make for breakfast. Amma told her that she had already made the *sambhar* and now she was going to make the *idlis*. This was a shock for Tanvi. Amma had soaked the rice and urad dal as soon as Tanvi had left for office. She had ground it in the evening.

Somu kept on gulping the soft spongy *idlis*. Tanvi looked at Somu and asked him to stop behaving like he has never eaten before.

"Tanvi I have packed your tiffin, carry it with you." Tanvi gave Amma a broad smile and quietly put the tiffin box in her bag.

Every day Amma made a new delicacy and Somu praised her to the skies. Amma had taken charge of Tanvi's entire house.

Tanvi compared her mother with Amma. Aai was so noninterfering in his sister-in-law's matters. Her Vahini had brought a new look to her parent's house. Aai never gave any suggestions to Namrata. Aai felt that now it was Namrata's turn to run the show.

Tanvi was fed up with the turmoil at home. One day she went directly to her mother's house after office.

Her mother was surprised to see her. The first thing she asked Tanvi was whether she had told Somu and Amma that she was coming home. Tanvi was very annoyed. "Do I need to take Somu's permission to come to your place? If you think so, I should leave." Aai caught hold of her hand and asked her to sit down. "Wait I will make *upma* for you." Tanvi settled on her favorite rocking chair. After all, this is the home where she was born. The home that was inhabited by Somu and his parents still had an alien feeling.

"Tanvi you must leave now. You must reach home what will your in-laws think?" said Aai.

Tanvi caught a *rikshaw* to go home. Tanvi realized that she was crying.

"I just can't handle things," she mumbled to herself. I never thought that Somu was such a mumma's boy.

Tanvi brushed her tears a side and combed her hair. She was afraid that Somu would bombard her with questions. But nothing of this sort happened. Tanvi went straight to her bedroom. She lay down on her bed. Somu called out loudly for her. She didn't respond to his calls. She thought he would come and ask her what was wrong with her.

Tanvi was feeling very tired and sick. Amma came to her room. "Are you not feeling well Tanvi?" Tanvi said she had a bad headache Amma brought some rice and *rasam* for her. "Don't go to sleep hungry Tanvi. Eat this you will feel better." Amma started feeding Tanvi with her hands. Tanvi felt very awkward. "It's ok I will eat." Tanvi pushed the rice and *rasam* in her mouth.

The next morning, Tanvi again felt very sick. She didn't have the energy to get up. She was feeling very dizzy. Somu had left early that morning. He had not even told Tanvi that he was leaving early.

Amma looked very concerned. "You rest at home today. Tanvi no need to go to office. Look at your eyes. They have sunk." Amma asked Tanvi the date of her last menstrual periods. Tanvi had not realized she had skipped her periods.

Amma realized this at once she started thanking Lord Venkateshwara in a heavy Tamil accent. There were tears in Amma's eyes. She embraced Tanvi. Tanvi thought "Oh God! I can't handle these Tamilians now one more to the gang."

Amma called Tanvi's mother to share the good news.

Amma said "Tanvi, we need to see the doctor first. Tanvi Ponnu. I am so happy." "Don't you worry Appa and I will stay back to look after you. Somu is very irresponsible I can't trust you with him in this condition."

"Ponnu let me know what you feel like eating." Tanvi was shocked with Amma's response. "God give me the strength to handle this situation." Tanvi prayed silently.

Mai

The phone had been ringing endlessly for some time. Priya reached for the receiver in the dark. “Is it Priya? Priya, this is Swati Mavshi calling from Pune.” Priya missed a heartbeat when she heard Swati Mavshi’s voice. Priya asked “Is Mai alright?” Swati responded “No Priya, I called you to inform you that Mai has suffered from a massive heart attack. We have got her admitted in a Cardiac Care Unit. I think you should start immediately.” Priya was shocked to hear this. Priya said “Don’t worry, I will leave by the first flight I get. Please take care of her. See that she gets the best treatment.” Priya was sweating profusely; she was feeling hot in London’s winter after hearing this news. Priya shook her husband to wake him up. Akshay was also shocked to hear what Priya told him. “It’s strange! I thought Mai had a strong heart. After all it had taken so many blows in the past. Priya start packing your bags. I will check if there are any tickets on the next flight to Mumbai.” Akshay managed to book a ticket for Priya from the net.

Priya wanted to take Ashish also along with her. Akshay said “Mai should be your priority now! Priya, you won’t be able to manage Ashish and Mai’s illness at the same time. Don’t worry I will look after him!” Priya felt that she had lost her ability to think. She mechanically carried out all the instructions that Akshay gave her.

Akshay handed over all the documents that were required for her travel. "Mai's friends will come and pick you up at the Mumbai airport Priya." Priya was constantly chanting the "Ganapati Atharvashish." "Only my prayers will help her! What else can I do from so far" she thought. Priya bid goodbye to Akshay and Ashish, her eight-year-old son.

"The journey is so long and my 'Mai' is so far" she said to herself. "I never thought that I would fly to India in such circumstances." Mai had never fallen sick before. At the most, she suffered from coughs and colds.

Priya was Mai's only daughter. Mai had single handedly bought up Priya. Priya's father had left both of them when Priya was about three or four years old. He had eloped away with a rich young widow. When she was growing up, Priya often questioned Mai about her father. Mai never answered her questions. When Priya grew up, she thought of dropping her father's name. Mai stopped her from doing it. "So remember Priya, how much ever you hate him don't forget he is your biological father, whatever few days he was with us, he cared for you." Priya was always perplexed with Mai's attitude. "Why didn't you stop him? Why didn't you fight for your rights Mai?"

"Priya may be he was right in his way. He met this lady after you were born. He thought he would lead a better life."

Her mother continued "I did not have any right to stop a person who was so engrossed in his selfish desires. Priya the day he told me he was seeing the other lady, I knew it was over between him and me. I constantly thank God that he didn't take you away from me." Priya was shocked when she heard these words from her mother. After that she never mentioned her father's name in front of Mai.

Priya remembered all the hardships Mai had to encounter to bring her up. Mai had not completed her graduation. Mai sold whatever little gold she had so that they could sustain for a few months.

Luckily Mai got a job of looking after an elderly Parsi couple in the upmarket camp area. Mr. and Mrs. Marolia, they had an outhouse in their bungalow. They allowed Mai and Priya to stay free of cost in their outhouse.

Mrs Marolia got Priya enrolled in one of the convent schools. Priya remembered how embarrassed she had felt when Mai came to attend any functions in school. Her mother was the simplest of the lot. The other mothers were draped in silks and chiffon sarees. Priya felt ashamed of herself when she remembered this.

The Marolias were really very helpful. Mrs Marolia asked Mai to educate herself if she wanted to earn well. Mai enrolled herself in a night collage. She worked throughout the day and attended college in the evening.

Mai managed to do her B.A. Mai worked in a school. She realized that she would get a better salary if she did her B.Ed. Mai completed her B.Ed. Mai got a good permanent job. Mai always felt indebted to the Marolias. Mr Marolia passed away the year Mai completed her B.Ed. It was as if he lived till Mai could manage things independently. Mrs Marolia went to live with her son in Mumbai. Mrs Marolia gave Mai a handsome amount of money for all the services she had rendered them. Priya remembered how helpless she and Mai had felt at that time. Mai had cried a lot when Mrs Marolia left them. "We have been orphaned in the real sense now," Mai said.

Priya and Mai moved to a small house in the same vicinity. Mai had to work very hard to look after herself and Priya. Mai completed each and every demand that Priya made. Whenever Priya pestered Mai to buy new clothes, Mai smiled and said "Who's going to look at me Priya? I can buy a few more books for you instead." How great is Mai? "Her world revolved only around me." Priya's eyes swelled with tears again. "Mai, Mai how could I be so selfish, you only thought about me and progress in life."

Just then, the airhostess asked her what she preferred "Tea or coffee?" Priya looked at her watch, it was past midnight in India. "God please save my Mai." The lady who was seated next to her sensed her uneasiness. "Is something wrong?" "No! Nothing" said Priya.

Priya conversed with the couple seated next to her. "I am going to see my mother in India, she has suffered a heart attack and she is hospitalized. My husband and son have stayed back. We live in Surrey. The couple too was from Surrey." They were surprised that they had not bumped into each other before. "Surrey is such a small place said the lady." The old man and his wife were traveling to India for the first time. Both of them were very excited. Priya told them the places they should see in Mumbai.

Priya pestered Mai to take her on a holiday. "Mai all my friends go to some place or the other. Why can't we go?" Poor Mai gave in to Priya's demands. God knows how! But Mai managed to take Priya to Goa. Mai had a distant cousin in Goa. Mai and Priya stayed with her in Ponda. Priya remembered how Bharati Mavshi and Mai had taken her to all the beaches and temples in Goa.

This was the only holiday that Priya and Mai ever had. After that Goa trip, Mai's cousin sister always came and spent a few days with them in Pune.

Priya was good in studies. She got very good grades in school. Mai's joy knew no bounds when Priya got admission in "Fergusson College." It was the most reputed college in Pune. Priya did her B.A. in economics from here. She graduated with honors. Priya had applied for a scholarship in the London School of Economics (LSE). Priya satisfied all the terms that were required for the scholarship. Mai and Priya were over the moon when they received an e-mail that Priya had got a scholarship. Priya was not sure whether she was doing the right thing. Mai stood like a rock of Gibraltar. "Priya you should consider yourself to be lucky that you will be studying in such a prestigious institution like LSE." Mai knew that Pandit Nehru, Dr Ambedkar and Mahatma Gandhi had studied here.

Mai said "Priya I can look after myself. Opportunity comes only once." Mai did all the necessary preparations to bid adieu to Priya. Priya remembered how strong Mai had been and she had not shed a single tear when Priya had left for London.

It was here in LSE that Priya met Akshay, her husband. It was really surprising that Akshay and Priya met here in London, though they were both from Pune.

Priya was scared to tell Mai about Akshay at first. Mai was very excited when she heard about Akshay. She wanted to meet him.

After completing their graduation in LSE, Akshay and Priya returned home for some time. Mai liked Akshay a lot. She found him to be very mature and understanding. Akshay's parents were skeptical about the proposal. They were a little uncomfortable as Priya's parents were separated. "What has her parents separation got to do with Priya?" Akshay was very adamant, so his parents had to give in.

Mai carried out all the marriage rituals as per Akshay's parent's desires. She had a large number of friends who helped her carry out all the functions successfully. Even Akshay's parents were surprised that Mai managed to do everything so efficiently at such short notice. Mai did not shed a single tear when Priya was going back to London. In fact, she told Akshay she had placed Priya in his safe hands so she didn't have to worry about her.

Just then, the airhostess made an announcement. "Passengers are requested to fasten their seat belts and be seated as we will be landing on Shivaji Chhatrapati Airport, Mumbai." Priya was happy that finally the long journey had come to an end.

Every time Priya came to Mumbai she remembered how Mai was waiting for her at the airport. She saw an elderly couple at the arrival gate with a placard for her. Priya failed to recognize them. They introduced themselves as Mr and Mrs Salunke. Mrs Salunke and Priya's Mai ran a crèche for working mothers. After Priya had left for London, she had no idea of Mai's friends and acquaintances. Priya was touched by the old couple's gesture. They had traveled all the way from Pune to pick her up at the airport.

"Why did you take so much trouble Kaka?" Priya asked. "Please don't think this way. My wife and I thought you will feel better if you have some company while you travel to Pune. Priya your Mai has helped us so much that we will never be able to repay back her kindness."

Mrs Salunke had brought *Dahi Bhaat* for her. "I know you must be tired. Eat something beta!"

Priya remembered how Mai always addressed her as "Priya beta." Priya realized she had not had a proper conversation with Mai in the past few days. Whenever Mai called she either was doing something for Ashish or was in a hurry to get ready for office.

They would converse with each other on Skype whenever Mai was free on the weekends. Ashish and Akshay would chat a lot with Mai. Priya was so engrossed in her own world that she didn't realize that she was the one who hardly spoke to Mai. On the way back, Mrs

Salunke told Priya that Mai collapsed when she was teaching in the crèche. “I was near her when she collapsed, I sensed that something was serious and I called for an ambulance. We took her to the hospital without wasting any time. Sorry Priya, we informed you a little late but we felt giving Mai medical help first was more important than informing you.”

“Let’s go straight to the hospital, I want to see Mai,” Priya burst out crying. She had controlled herself for a long time.

They reached the hospital where Mai was admitted. Priya changed and entered the CCU were Mai was sleeping peacefully with an oxygen mask over her face. Priya called out softly “Mai.” Mai opened her eyes and smiled at Priya behind the oxygen mask. Mai signaled asking for Ashish. “I have left him with Akshay.” Mai tried to remove the oxygen mask. She wanted to talk to Priya. The nurse came and put the mask back and she asked Mai to keep quiet. The nurse signaled Priya not to talk to Mai. Priya just held her Mai’s hand. She caressed Mai’s hand slowly. Mai had an I.V. attached to her. Priya kissed Mai’s other hand. She saw Mai smile behind the mask. The nurse came again and asked Priya to come to the side room. Dr Dudani who was treating Mai wanted to have a word with Priya. Dr Dudani was a tall handsome, middle-aged doctor. “I understand that you are Mrs Ulka’s daughter. She has had a massive myocardial infarct. It’s really very surprising how she could sustain such a big injury to the heart. The infarct has damaged a major part of heart muscles. We are giving her the best possible treatment available, but the next forty-eight hours are critical.”

Priya was too dumbfounded to understand anything. She thanked the doctor and his team for looking after her Mai in her absence.

Priya came outside the CCU to look for Mr and Mrs Salunke who were waiting for her. Priya was mobbed by ten to twelve people who were asking her about Mai. Priya was very surprised to see so many people standing outside the CCU for her Mai. Priya did not know half of the people. Swati Mavshi introduced her to all the people around her. "Don't worry Priya. Mai will overcome this. She is an angel. Mai is always there when anyone needs help. She is a fighter, she will come out." Priya's heart swelled with pride when she heard these words about Mai. Everybody had something to say about Mai. "She was like my mother Priya" said a young girl. "She prevented mc from committing suicide when I had lost all desire to live when my husband left me. I stayed with her for some days till I came back to normal."

Priya interacted with the people outside the CCU for an hour. Swati Mavshi asked Priya to go home and take rest for some time.

Priya was surprised to see her Mai's house so clean. Everything was in place. Priya and Ashish's photographs were placed on an old table.

Swati Mavshi had kept "*Pohe*" ready for Priya just like Mai. Swati Mavshi was Mai's oldest and best friend. Priya had a quick bath and she rushed back to the hospital. She did not want to stay away for a minute also from Mai.

Priya realized how old Mai had become. "I never realized that Mai was aging" Priya thought. Priya noticed the freckles on her face. This was something new about Mai. Priya wanted to talk to Mai. "Mai you get well soon and then we can talk to each other till the early hours in the morning."

Priya heard Mai, "Priya, don't worry I will not leave you and go. Even if I go my soul will always remain with you." Suddenly, the monitors beeped. Priya felt Mai's hand. It was cold. Mai's breathing was shallow. Priya was whisked away. The doctors tried to resuscitate Mai. Her inotropic support was increased but Mai's heart had stopped responding. "My soul will always be with you beta." These words were echoing in Priya's ears.

Dark Secret

Shraddha and Arjun had just returned from a holiday in Spain. Shraddha said "Arjun, I won't be able to get back to the same routine. How I wish life was just a long holiday with no tensions."

Arjun responded "C'mon Shraddha stop dreaming now. I have a photo shoot in the evening. Shraddha make something simple for breakfast. Just some simple *subji* and *roti*. I am dying to eat home-made food." Shraddha exclaimed "Subji roti for breakfast!" Shraddha reminded Arjun that there were no vegetables in the house. The house had been locked for a week. Shraddha said "I can make coffee and toast for you." Arjun didn't want to argue with Shraddha It was their first holiday overseas. Shraddha and Arjun had gone for a honeymoon after three years of marriage. They couldn't afford one as soon as they got married.

Shraddha said "Arjun, I think Spain is the ultimate destination. I am in love with Madrid. It was worth the wait." Arjun, ever the spoilsport, said "C'mon Shraddha, our holiday is over. Let's come back to normal."

How can this man switch on and switch off so fast? "Arjun, we should have stayed for a few more days."

Arjun just shook Shraddha to bring her back to normal. Shraddha stamped her feet and entered the kitchen.

God! The house smelled awful, since it was closed for a week. The worst thing was to get back to normal routine life. Arjun was ready. He had black coffee and toast. "I will be back by 7.30 or 8 pm. Do the unpacking and call Ma."

Arjun grabbed his car keys and left. Shraddha called her Aai. She spoke at length about Madrid. "I actually saw the places where most of the Hindi songs are shot." Aai listened to all her stories patiently.

Shraddha's Aai said "Why don't you come home Shraddha? From tomorrow, you will join work. You will be busy as usual. Come home for lunch." Shraddha agreed at once. "Aai please make my favorite goan curry and rice." Aai said "Shraddha you don't have to tell me. What to make? I have nice Pomfret in the fridge."

Shraddha organized her house, refilled her refrigerator and she called her maid. Both of them set the house as usual. "Home is Sweet Home." Only the household chores are boring.

Shraddha reached her mother's place. She hugged her mother tightly. Shraddha relished the fish curry and rice and stretched on the sofa in the living room.

"Shraddha, it's three years since you are married. You must start a family dear. See all your friends have children. You are the only one left behind, 'Kalji Vatte' Why don't you see a doctor?" Shraddha said "Aai, chill. All these years we were using contraceptives. Now we are settled. In fact, Arjun and I have discussed this. Don't worry Aai?"

"Goodness gracious! Aai I need to go back home. It's 7 pm. I need to reach home before Arjun comes."

Arjun was a well-known model now. Arjun was very good looking. He had a great physique. Shraddha and Arjun were friends since childhood. They had grown up together. Both of them had come a long way.

They had made it big on their own. Shraddha too used to do modeling assignments. There was so much uncertainty in this field that they decided that one of them should have a steady income. Shraddha had done a course in travel and tourism. She took up a job in a well-known travel agency. Her boss was a Parsi lady Mrs Pastonji.

"I have to call up Ma." Shraddha called up Ma to tell her that they were back. "Shraddha you reached early in the morning and you are calling me know?" Ma always found faults in Shraddha. Shraddha asked "Did Arjun call you?" Ma responded "No, he must be busy." "I like that," Shraddha mumbled to herself.

Thank God we don't stay together. Shraddha really pitied the girls staying with their mothers-in-law. Shraddha thought "I can't have a decent conversation even on the phone."

Arjun called and said he would be late. Shraddha was disappointed. "Arjun you should have told this early. I could have spent some more time with Aai."

It was three months since they had come back from Spain. Every month when Shraddha realized that she did not conceive, she would feel very sad.

"Arjun, I think we should see a doctor." Finally, Shraddha and Arjun took an appointment with a well-known doctor. Shraddha and Arjun told the doctor that they had taken contraceptive care for a long time and it was only three months since they were trying to conceive. "Give yourself some more time." This was the doctor's advice.

Shraddha was not satisfied with the doctor's explanation. "Arjun, she should have advised some tests at least." "Shut up Shraddha, you think you are smarter than the doctor. Shraddha, you are obsessed with this baby business." Shraddha explained "Arjun nobody says anything to you. Everybody asks me." Arjun snapped "Shraddha, it is our decision as to when we should have a child. Nobody has a right to poke their noses in our private life." Shraddha said angrily "Arjun, why don't you talk sternly to your Ma. Like you talk to me. Every time she talks only about one thing, when is the stork visiting. Even people in my office have started asking me now."

Arjun said impatiently "Shraddha, don't over react. My mother is concerned. She asks me also the same question. After all, she is my mom. It's only this that she is a little more concerned about us."

Shraddha had tears in her eyes. "Arjun, even you think I am at fault." Arjun held Shraddha. "Shraddha stop blaming yourself. Let's give ourselves some time. What's wrong with you? It's not the end of the world."

The next day Shraddha spoke to her Aai. "Every time Arjun's mother calls me, she taunts me." Shraddha's Aai asked her to come with her to her old gynecologist. "Shraddha, you were born there. I trust Dr Desai a lot." When Shraddha and her mother went to the doctor's clinic, Dr Desai who was her mother gynecologist was not there. Instead, they saw his son Dr Milind.

Shraddha found Dr Milind very charming. She developed a liking for him immediately. Dr Milind asked Shraddha to come with Arjun. Shraddha's mother asked Dr Milind to take over Shraddha's responsibility and to look after her like his own sister. "Doctor, I have a lot of trust in your family and your father." Dr Milind assured Shraddha's mother that she should not worry.

Shraddha's Aai said "Look Shraddha I have shown you the best doctor that I know. Now you come with your husband and do as he says."

Arjun and Shraddha went to Dr Milind's clinic the following week. Dr Milind spoke at Iength to them. "First of all you need to remain relaxed and calm." Arjun interrupted "Doctor, you need to tell Shraddha this, I am absolutely cool about this. These days Shraddha is very temperamental, she loses her cool very easily." The doctor did an internal examination for Shraddha and asked her the details of her menstrual history.

Then the doctor said "First and foremost we need to do your semen analysis. Mr Arjun in Infertility it is always gents first, whereas everywhere it is ladies first." Arjun laughed out aloud at the doctor's statement.

Arjun went to the laboratory as he was directed. He thought "God what is all this. Is being a father so difficult? Cats and dogs also conceive easily. Why are we having difficulties?" First time, Arjun felt nervous. Arjun was a very confident person otherwise. It was his confidence that had made him a successful model.

Arjun was very surprised when the receptionist in the laboratory handed over a playboy magazine to him. "Sir, this will help you." Arjun was surprised with her attitude. Maybe this is a part of her job, so she gives the instructions mechanically.

"When should I come to collect the reports?" he asked. The receptionist said "You can come and collect them in the evening." Arjun said "My wife will come and collect them, is it OK?" The receptionist answered "Tell her to bring the receipt sir." The same evening, Shraddha went to the lab to collect the report.

Out of curiosity, she opened the report and saw the sperm count report, nil. Shraddha couldn't understand anything. She spoke to the pathologist. The pathologist asked her to see Dr Milind.

Dr Milind was held up in an emergency. Shraddha waited patiently for two hours to talk to him. There was another patient who was also waiting to meet Dr Milind. "I have an emergency" she said. "I have to get an abortion done. God knows how I have conceived despite taking all precautions. This is nature's injustice," she said. Shraddha thought "Here I am dying to be a mother and someone is trying to abort an unwanted child." Finally, her wait was over. Dr Milind came to his consulting after the emergency cesarean section.

Shraddha handed the report to Dr Milind. He became grim the moment he saw the report. "Shraddha, this condition is known as azoospermia, that is, absence of sperms."

"We have to find out the reason for it. Why don't you bring Arjun to the clinic tomorrow." Shraddha agreed to do so. Shraddha was intelligent enough to understand the meaning of azoospermia.

She immediately typed "Azoospermia" on Google. Google was a boon at times but today Google gave Shraddha information, which made her restless. Shraddha contemplated whether to tell Arjun about this information. Arjun called her to remind her to collect his lab report. Shraddha feigned that she had forgotten to do so. Arjun said "Go and collect the reports before the lab closes." Shraddha prayed "Oh God! How could you play such a cruel joke on me?"

She thought "What if the reports have changed? How come I didn't think of this? How can a macho looking man like Arjun be azoospermic? I will convince Arjun to do a semen analysis from another lab." Shraddha had Dr Milind's cell number. It was almost 9:30 pm. At the most he would be annoyed to get a call this late. Dr Milind was at a social party. Shraddha could hear loud music in the background. Shraddha apologized to him and asked him if they should get another report done again. "You can Shraddha, but there has to be abstinence for three days."

"It's ok doctor. I will see you with the next report."

Arjun enquired about his reports. Shraddha said that he had azoospermia. Arjun failed to understand what Shraddha meant. Shraddha told Arjun that the doctor had asked her to get the reports done from another lab.

Arjun said "Please Shraddha why don't you talk to Dr Milind. It's a torture." Shraddha was feeling very bad she was lying to Arjun. It was the first time she had done this. Shraddha pacified Arjun and finally Arjun gave in. After three days, Arjun went through the same thing. This time, the lab was different.

This lab also showed the same results. The same evening Shraddha and Arjun went to meet Dr Milind. Dr Milind greeted them with his thousand watt smile. Patiently, Dr Milind explained the meaning of azoospermia to Arjun. Arjun couldn't believe what Dr Milind was saying. "Dr Milind, are there no hopes at all?" asked Shraddha. The doctor spoke "Medical science has advanced so much that there is treatment for everything. We need to do things stepwise. Do you jump to get to the top-most floor in a building? You need to ascend stepwise. It's the same with treatment. It's a game of patience and belief in yourself and your doctor." Arjun's eyes swelled with tears. Both Shraddha and Arjun broke down. Dr Milind comforted both of them. "See all of us need to work together with understanding and trust. Tomorrow we get some blood tests and ultrasound done for Mr Arjun." Arjun responded "I will do whatever you say doctor." Dr Milind also felt very bad for Arjun. It was his experience that male infertility was more traumatic for a couple.

All the tests didn't give any satisfactory answer. What do we do now?

Dr Milind spoke very slowly and cautiously. "Listen Shraddha and Arjun. Have you heard about AID?" Both of them had not heard the term before.

"Well, I will explain. AID means Artificial Insemination Donor, which means that we take a donor sample of semen and instill it directly into the woman's uterus. Conception takes place and the woman gets pregnant. We do this provided both of you are willing for this. Only three of us will know this. Both of you think about it and come back to me." They asked "Doctor, are there couples like us who have done this?" The doctor answered "I have done this for a number of my patients."

They had more doubts. "Will anyone come to know about this?" The doctor answered "How will anyone come to know unless you tell them about it? I have told you an option. Both of you as a couple have to take a decision. Take your time and come and see me."

Shraddha and Arjun left the doctor's clinic. Both were devastated. Shraddha was crying profusely. "Arjun we have never ever thought or wished bad for any one, why are we going through this?" Arjun was too shocked to answer anything. "Shraddha you can leave me. You deserve a better life. I know how eager you are to be a mother." Shraddha said "Are you crazy Arjun? We have been together always. I will stay with you. It doesn't matter if I cannot be a mother. So what Arjun? We will live lavishly every six months. We will go for a holiday." Shraddha was trying to put on a bold act.

Both of them had a quiet dinner. They could hardly eat. Shraddha and Arjun were tossing and turning in bed throughout the night. "We are not interested in having children. That's what we will say when people ask us."

Shraddha and Arjun got back to their routine. "Arjun's mother would constantly pester them with the same question. Why don't you tell her the truth Shraddha? At least it will stop her from torturing us."

Shraddha once asked "Arjun why don't we follow what Dr Milind has told us." Arjun replied "Actually, Shraddha I was also thinking on those grounds but I didn't have the courage to talk to you." Shraddha said "Arjun, I am absolutely ok if you have no problems." Both of them hugged each other.

Dr Milind explained the procedure in detail to both of them. He took their consent on a consent form. He told them the legal angle also. "How many times do we have to do this?" they asked.

"Well, if you are lucky you can conceive in the first cycle. Otherwise, we can try up to three cycles."

The treatment began as per the doctor's instructions. Shraddha could only pray. Arjun would fix his appointment for shoots as per Shraddha's treatment schedule and timings. "This is the least. I can do." Shraddha had never seen Arjun to be so submissive.

The doctor said "Now we only have to wait and watch. Come and see me if you skip your menses." Shraddha asked "What if I get them?" The doctor said "Come and see me on the second day."

Shraddha kept her fingers crossed. "God please, please help us." She thought "If I don't skip my menses both Arjun and I will be very disappointed ."

Dr Milind assured them that they should try the same thing again. "Remember that we are going against nature so it will take some time." Shraddha thought "May be God also does not want me to carry someone else's child. What am I thinking?" She pinched herself to come back to normal.

Shraddha went through the same ordeal that she had gone through last month. This time she cautioned herself again and again. Finally, she skipped her cycle. Shraddha was so eager that she brought home a home pregnancy kit and did her pregnancy test. Her pregnancy test was positive. Arjun and Shraddha were overjoyed.

The first trimester was at first a little difficult to handle. Shraddha experienced a lot of nausea and vomiting. Arjun's Ma came to live with them. Arjun's mother was so overjoyed that she took utmost care of Shraddha. Shraddha used to wonder where her old mother-in-law had gone. She lived with Shraddha throughout the pregnancy. Finally, the day arrived when Shraddha delivered a healthy baby girl. Arjun's mother held her grandchild in her arms. "Arjun she looks exactly like you. She has your eyes and nose." Shraddha and Arjun were gleaming with pride. There were tears rolling down Shraddha's cheeks when she heard her mother-in-law's remarks.

Ordinary to Extraordinary

Anita was an average looking girl. She belonged to a middle class family. She was the second child among three children. Her father, Chavan, was a senior clerk in the Zilla Parishad and her mother was a teacher.

Anita's parents were very disheartened when she was born. They were hoping for a boy. Anita was very understanding from childhood. Her elder sister was the pampered daughter. Sushmita was good in studies. Her younger brother Rohan was also pampered because he was the son of the family.

Anita was just average in studies. The situation at home, made her very understanding and mature at a very early age. Many times Anita managed on things that were passed over by her sister Sushmita.

In school, she used Sushmita's old books. At home, she used the clothes that were passed over by her sister. Anita altered Sushmita's clothes, she put some lace or attached something new to the old clothes and gave it a new look. Anita never complained or asked for anything for herself. Sushmita never helped her mother in any of the household chores. She shied away from doing anything under the pretext of studies. Anita's mother always discriminated between her and Sushmita. Anita's father made up for her mother's behavior. She was his favorite daughter. Sushmita's dreams were big, whereas Anita's aims were very ordinary. Sushmita was very selfish. She never compromised. Anita willingly did everything at home. Anita kept the house clean and tidy. She helped her younger brother in all his assignments and she always helped Sushmita. Sushmita completed her journals with the help of Anita. Anita always believed in helping everybody. Even in the neighborhood, the aunties asked Anita for help. Anita willingly helped everyone. If someone was sick in the neighborhood, Anita was the first person to nurse the sick. If there were guests coming, Anita was the first to help with the cooking. Anita was loved and wanted by everyone.

Sushmita got very good marks in the twelfth standard. She got admission for engineering in College of Engineering, Pune. Sushmita's parents were over the moon. Anita settled for graduation in arts. Her parents also didn't force her to take up any lucrative course. Both Anna and Aai were of the opinion that Anita's temperament was not made for any profession. "She will make a very good housewife," Aai's constan remark.

Anita too never took studies very seriously but she wanted to do a course in fashion designing. She had often expressed her desire to Aai and Anna. "Complete your graduation, then we shall see" said her mother. Meanwhile, Sushmita completed her B.E. with flying colors and like all engineers she too wanted to go to United States to get a master's degree.

Sushmita got admission for M.S. in “Old Dominion.” It was a well-known university in Norfolk in Virginia. The entire family was overjoyed when they heard of Sushmita’s achievement.

Anna said that in the past seven generations no one from their family had traveled beyond the shores of Mumbai. Sushmita’s parents left no stone unturned for Sushmita’s admission. They had to show a handsome amount in their bank account. Anna and Aai took a loan to show such a big amount in their account. This was one of the terms that had to be fulfilled for Sushmita’s stay abroad. Finally, the family managed to fulfill all the clauses that were required for Sushmita to go to the university in USA. Anna had taken one month leave to complete all the formalities that were required. Finally, the family bid farewell to Sushmita. Sushmita left her hometown with great dreams in her eyes.

The idea of Anita studying fashion designing was dropped. This was due to financial pressure of sending Sushmita abroad for her studies. Her mother said “In fact, Anita you too should start looking for a job. We are in a financial crisis now.” Luckily Rohan was in school and so they had some time before he took up a professional course.

Just when Anita started looking for a job, a neighbor brought a marriage proposal for her. Anita’s Anna was not ready to get her married so early, but her Aai was very happy as someone had come on their own with a proposal.

Anita's Aai convinced her father to accept the proposal. Girish was a decent boy. He worked as an accountant in a private company. Girish liked Anita and was willing to marry Anita. Anita was confused. She didn't know what to do. At the same time, she didn't want to hurt her mother. Anita's mother liked Girish all the more because he did not ask for any dowry and did not make any demands.

Girish's parents were simple people who did farming in a village called Madha near Solapur. Girish was their only son. He had three sisters. Two of them were married and his younger sister was studying.

Anita and Girish got married in a very simple ceremony. Sushmita did not attend her wedding. She could not afford to travel to India.

Anita moved into a rented house after getting married to Girish. Girish wanted to give Anita a lot of comforts but he couldn't do so. He had to manage a lot of things in the meager salary he got. Girish tried to keep Anita happy by doing small gestures like buying her a *gajra* or taking her for a ride on his scooter. Their marriage was a union of the two most compromising and helpful people. Anita's mother started understanding her value after she got married. She understood how helpful her daughter was. She realized that it was only because of Anita that their house functioned well. Anna too realized that Anita had been the backbone of their family.

Within a year, Anita was the mother of a baby girl. Both Anita and Girish were overjoyed at the birth of their daughter. They named her Asmita, which meant pride.

With one more addition in the family, Anita found it very difficult to make both ends meet. She couldn't work full-time as there was no one to look after Asmita. Anita started doing small alteration jobs at home. Within a month's time she got a fair amount of money. She started doing tailoring at home.

Anita received many orders. Anita always created new and smart designs. She stitched clothes in such a manner that even clothes made from any ordinary cloth looked chic and smart. Anita's stitching skills became famous and soon she got a lot of orders. Within a year's time, Anita hired two assistants to help her. Girish had given a very important tip to Anita. "Charge a little less than what other people charge. This will give you volumes of work. You can try different ideas, different designs for your clients. If the clients don't like you your creation, they will not argue much because you are not charging them a lot."

Anita shifted her working base to a rented place in a shopping mall. Girish asked her to take professional help to do the interiors of her shop. Girish told her that without investing they would not get profits. He helped her secure a loan for the new venture. Everything moved at a very quick pace. Anita hired tailors from Uttar Pradesh. They were very good in their craft. Her outlet was named "Ordinary to Extraordinary." Girish asked her to make a logo for her outlet. O&E was the logo on her signboard.

Anita just couldn't believe that this was happening to her. She had never thought in her wildest dreams that a venture that was started with the intention of sharing financial responsibility with Girish would turn out to be such a great success. Anita's O&E got a lot of recognition. People traveled across the city to get their dresses tailored from Anita. Anita realized that she would earn more profits if she made clothes instead of running only a tailoring outlet.

She decided to keep her tailoring outlet as it is and buy a new shop and start a boutique. Girish said "I am very impressed with your idea of starting a boutique." Anita asked "Girish, Would you quit your job and join as a financial advisor in this new venture?" Girish said "I will be very happy to do so. This is a great idea. Anita, you should concentrate more on the creativity and I will look after the finances."

Girish came up with a bright idea that they should open three or four outlets in different parts of the city. If they opened outlets all over the city, they would cater to all clients across the city.

Anita was a little scared of taking such a big financial leap but Girish convinced her to do so. He said "You and your team concentrate only on the creativity. I shall look into the marketing strategies."

Girish made huge hoardings all over the place. He made young aspiring models to be the face of O&E. Girish worked very hard to promote O&E as a brand. Anita's and Girish's efforts gave results within a year's time.

Their O&E label became well known in Pune.

They moved from their rented house into a new flat in a posh locality.

Their hard working nature helped her a lot. They worked from morning till night. Every month, she created a new collection. Anita came from a middle class background. She knew exactly what people wanted in return for the money they paid.

Girish wanted Anita to create bold designs. Girish asked "Anita, please create designs in silk and chiffon material, which is the choice of the upmarket people." Anita and her team had an idea to hold an exhibition first to get a feel of the taste of the higher society clients.

Girish also found Anita's idea of an exhibition very enterprising.

Anita and her team worked for six whole months for the exhibition. Anita designed *kurtis, lehengas and cholis*. She created lovely gowns and *kaflans*. Anita's exhibition was to be held in one of the five stars in the city. Girish had booked the majestique hall in one of the five star hotels for a week. Anita's creations were such a hit that all her clothes sold within three days.

This gave them confidence. Girish was very happy with Anita's achievements. Girish too improved his marketing skills. His strategies were very clear. He believed that advertising played a big role in the fashion industry. Now they employed an advertising firm to take care of the advertising for their O&E.

The ad man came with a perfect punchline. "O&E for the Ordinary. O&E for the Extraordinary."

Anita was now no longer a local designer. She catered to the rich and famous.

Anita's boutiques were spread all across Pune. Girish had plans to open outlets all across Maharashtra. Anita's firm was taking giant leaps now.

Girish and Anita not only made life comfortable for themselves, but they also gifted a car to Anita's parents.

Anita's Aai was all praises for Anita now. She often said that it was because of her decision of getting Anita married at an early age, Anita tasted success at an early age. The adversity and financial crisis had made her take up tailoring. Anita's success story was written in many newspapers and magazines. Girish often teased and said that it was Anita's mother's vision that had made her so successful.

Anita's mother was so stupid that she never understood the underlying meaning.

Sushmita completed her master's degree. She didn't get a job immediately as there was economic recession in USA. She had to do odd jobs to sustain herself. She met Yogesh at the "Old Dominion." They went around for some time. She finally broke the news of her relationship with Yogesh. Both of them decided to get married in USA. Sushmita's parents were undecided whether to go or not to go. Anita brought tickets for Aai and Anna so that they could attend Sushmita's wedding.

"It's an important day in her life. She will miss you" she said.

Sushmita knew of Anita's success but she did not know how well she was doing. Anna and Aai regaled Sushmita with Anita's stories. Aai continuously praised Anita. "You should see her boutiques Sushmita. All her clients come in big cars. You should see how the rich ladies beg Anita to design clothes for them."

Anna had even carried all the magazines and paper cuttings that had Anita's articles.

Sushmita was also proud and happy for Anita. Sushmita had to do all the household work herself. This was something which Sushmita had never done before. Sushmita had to cook and clean. She had to reach her office in time.

Sushmita's parents too realized how difficult things were for her. "This was her choice" Anna said when he was leaving for India.

Sushmita became pregnant. She asked her parents to come and help her. Sushmita's mother went back again to help her. Sushmita's Aai found it very difficult to look after Sushmita, the baby and the house.

Aai realized how thoughtful Anita had been. Poor Anita had delivered in a government hospital because she didn't want her parents to bear the cost of a delivery in a private hospital. The day Asmita was a month old, Anita had gone back to her husband's house.

Sushmita had never ever bothered to ask how Anita was doing. In those days, Anita called Aai and Sushmita twice a day to find out how they were doing.

Anita was doing so well but she still had her feet planted firmly on the ground.

Anita and Girish had adopted ten girls from an orphanage. They took responsibility of these girls in every way.

Even if Anita was busy she personally looked after Asmita. She took Asmita with her wherever she went. She always saw to it that Asmita was growing up with the right values.

Sushmita was fed up with her life in the United States. She always compared herself with Anita. She always said that Anita had name, fame and money. She enjoyed everything all the more because she was among family and friends.

One day Anita received Sushmita's call in the middle of the night. "Anita, will you please give me a job in your O&E. I am fed up. I want to come back to my people and my roots."

Anita said "Sushmita, you are most welcome to join me. But Sushmita, will you like working under me?"

Anita heard the phone getting disconnected. Whether it got disconnected or was disconnected was to be understood.

Responsibility

The alarm buzzed at 5.30 am. Malvika switched it off and went to sleep. Avinash shook her and asked her to get up at once. "Malvika, get up or else you won't be able to get the children ready for school." Malvika yawned and got out of her bed. She had a severe backache. Malvika had still not got over yesterday's fatigue and a new day had already begun.

Avinash made tea for both of them. This was his only contribution to help Malvika throughout the day.

Malvika made breakfast for her children. She called out for Aditya. When she did not get a response, she went to the children's bedroom. Aditya pulled the quilt over his face and slept again. Avni sat up in her bed and started crying. Malvika pulled her close and asked her why she was crying. "Ma I forgot to do my Marathi homework. I have four pages to write. If I don't do my homework, I will get no marks." Malvika said "Why don't you do your homework on time? How many times did I remind you yesterday? Nobody wants to listen to me. You forget everything when you start watching the stupid reality shows on TV." Avni listened and then ran to her study table and started doing her homework.

Aditya reminded her to sign his test papers. "Ma, its quarter to eight, I have to brush my teeth and have a bath." Malvika grabbed Avni's pencil and started completing her work. "Ma, write like me otherwise my teacher will shout at me." Malvika said "You are scared of your teacher. Why don't you feel scared of me?"

At 8:15 am, the rickshaw kaka came. Malvika managed to send the children in time. Just then Avinash returned from his morning work.

Malvika sighed in relief. Avinash said "Malvika you have made the children idle, you do everything for them. Tell me, didn't we get ready to go to school. You pamper them. Aditya is a grown up boy, but he won't do a single thing. Avni, I understand, is young. Why don't you train them properly to do things on their own? I am telling you both of them are useless. It's your fault Malvika." Malvika said "You don't help me at all. As a father it is your duty also to discipline them. Every day, I face a new difficulty when I get up and get them ready before going to office. If I leave things to be done by then, they will never reach school in time. We must thank our stars that our rikshaw kaka is considerate. He waits at least. Other rikshaw fellows just honk and leave, they don't bother whether the children are ready or not."

"Ok! Ok get my breakfast ready." Avinash had only a bowl of sprouts every day for breakfast. "How can this man have the same boring breakfast every day?" Malvika made a big mug of tea for herself. She dipped two slices of bread that had heaps of Amul butter in it.

"Malvika, how can you eat this. You don't exercise, you don't bother about your diet. You don't bother about your looks. It's useless talking to you Malvika." Malvika turned a deaf hear to Avi's talk and had her breakfast. "Malvika have a look at what you are wearing. Your gown is faded. Malvika why don't you think about your avatar at home." Malvika said "I am fed up with you. I am a mother of two." Avinash said "I don't expect you to look neat and tidy all the time but at least remain presentable. Your whole world rotates around the children and food. Do I make any unnecessary demands from you?"

Tears started flowing down Malvika's cheeks. She really lost her temper. "Avinash, I am constantly running about. If I start being selfish and start thinking only about myself and my looks, all of you will remain hungry. A simple breakfast. You, you need only sprouts; your son Prince Aditya eats only omelet toast and princess Avani has nothing that is ready. She will always have something other than what is ready. I put up with all your whims and fancies. What do I get in return? Forget the compliments. All you can do is criticize."

Avinash left the house in a hurry. He didn't find his car keys but he didn't ask for Malvika's help. "Malvika I am going to Calcutta tomorrow. I will be away for a week." Malvika didn't react to this statement. She cleared the table and ran to get ready to go to office. Malvika had a lot of work in the office. She had a heap of files to clear today. The day just flew away.

The lift was not working so she had to walk to the parking space. She dragged her Kinetic Honda out of the parking lot.

There was so much of traffic on the road. Driving was no longer easy. As she was waiting at a signal, she saw a fruit vendor selling fruits on the other side of the road. There are no fruits in the house. She parked her scooter and walked to the other side. She purchased the fruits in dozens. She thought "I don't have to bother for one week now." She brought the fruits at a cheaper rate than what the fruit seller had quoted. "Bargaining is an art" she said to herself.

Just as she was crossing the road a motorcycle came from behind and pushed her very badly. She was saved because of the helmet. She fell down with a big bang. Malvika had forgotten to remove her helmet while she was crossing the road. The helmet proved to be a blessing in disguise.

She fell flat, she was feeling very giddy. She was experiencing excruciating pain in her hands. She tried to get up. She couldn't get up. A mob gathered around her. A lady helped her to get up. Someone gave her water to drink. The young boy who was responsible for the accident came forward to help her. Just then Malvika's office colleague happened to see her. Mrs Samta, her colleague, was shocked to see Malvika hurt. Mrs Samta called Avinash and told him about Malvika's accident.

Malvika was taken to a nearby hospital for treatment. Malvika had fractured her hand, her ulnar bone had a crack, her leg had sprained. Malvika's hand had to be plastered and her leg was tied with a crepe bandage. Aditya and Avni reached the hospital with their neighbors. The children were very scared. Avni started crying loudly when she saw her mother. Aditya put on a brave front. He took out his handkerchief and wiped the sweat across Malvika's forehead. "Don't worry Ma you will be alright. Is the pain very severe?" Just then, Avinash stepped in. "What happened? How many times I have told you stop driving your two wheeler? How could you be so careless?" Aditya interrupted, "daddy she was hit by a motorcycle when she was crossing the road. She was not driving." Malvika said "Avinash there were no fruits in the house so I parked my scooter and walked to the fruit stall on the other side of the road." The boy who was responsible for Malvika's accident came forward. "Sir, I lost control over my bike and I dashed against madam."

"Sir, I will bear the hospital expenses but please don't lodge an FIR against me. I have exams next week, I am in the final year. This will affect my career. Sir!"

The young boy started pleading. Malvika signaled Avinash and asked him to forgive the young fellow. Avinash put his hands around the young fellow's shoulders and asked him to calm down. "It's Ok, but you better be more careful while driving."

Aditya asked the doctor the details of the medicines to be given to Malvika. Malvika was feeling much better now. Avinash and Aditya helped Malvika walk up to the car. Aditi was holding Malvika's purse in one hand and her broken sandals on the other hand.

Aditya kept asking Malvika if she was alright. As soon as they reached home, Aditya pulled a small table near the sofa. He made Malvika lie on the sofa with her feet up on the table. Aditya brought pillows from inside. He tried to make his Ma comfortable.

Aditya made a cup of tea for Malvika. Avinash ordered food from outside for them. Avinash made a drink for himself. Avinash just needed a reason to have a drink.

Aditya asked Avni to do her homework. Avinash was very disturbed he couldn't cancel his Calcutta trip. How could he leave Malvika like this?

His parents had gone on a pilgrimage. He was trying desperately to contact them. Malvika's parents had gone to Australia to visit her brother..

Malvika was in great pain. Avinash asked "Is it very painful Malu? Eat something and then you can take your pain-killers. Why do you burn yourself so much Malvika? It's Ok. We could have done without fruits. See what the fruits have cost us. What if anything had happened to you Malu? I need you, the kids need you." Avinash was shaken up very badly.

Just then the food parcel arrived. Aditya and Avinash emptied the food into their utensils. Aditya served Malvika food in the hall. He gave her, her dose of medicines. He gave Malvika a finger bowl to wash her hands.

"Daddy, it's ok. If you cannot cancel your tour I will bunk school and stay back with Ma. We will ask the maid to make food. Avni will go to school so you don't have to worry about her."

Both Malvika and Avinash were shocked. They could not believe it was their Aditya behaving so responsibly. “Look Malvika, look at my son. How responsible he is. You just keep on complaining.” Avinash looked proudly at his son. Malvika couldn’t believe her ears to hear such things from Avinash.

Portrait

Seemantini had stayed awake the entire night. She was keen on completing the painting she had started. Her dress was crumpled and smudged with paint. Seema concentrated on getting the right look on the lady's face. "She needs to look a little bit more realistic. I think I should give her lips a little more lighter shade." Seema started mixing new colors in her palette.

Just then Shailesh entered the studio. "Wow! Seema you have made a masterpiece. The lady on the canvas looks so real, I feel as if she is going to talk to me." Seema gave him a crooked smile. "Are you sure of what you are talking Shailesh?" Shailesh responded "Yeah! I am sure, this is surely one of your best paintings. Seema, why don't you have a quick wash. Look! I have brought tea for you. Just tell me when are you going to stop working nonstop for so many hours. I really wonder how you can paint continuously for so many hours. Don't you feel tired? Seema you have been up the entire night. Don't do this. Eat something and go to sleep." Seema responded "I won't be able to sleep till I get the right expression on my subject's face." Shailesh said "Seema it's useless talking to you. I may not be a good artist but I understand a little bit of art. Don't do anything now. The painting is complete. If you try to overcorrect it you will spoil it, all your efforts will go vain." Seema stood at a distance and saw her painting from all angles. "What you say is right Shailesh. I was wondering if I should give the lips a little more correction, but what you say makes sense."

Seemantini and Shailesh had a live-in relationship. Both of them had graduated in fine arts. Seema was a very good painter. She concentrated on her paintings. Shailesh worked as a commercial artist. Shailesh worked with all the leading advertising agencies. Shailesh was very happy with what he was doing. He was happy that he was living life as he wanted to.

Seema had worked very hard to establish her name in the world of painters. Her artwork was getting recognition slowly and steadily. Seema had worked day and night to complete her paintings. Her life revolved around her canvas and paints.

Seema came from a conservative family. Her parents did not approve of her relationship with Shailesh. Her parents also did not approve of the path she had chosen as a career. One day after a heated argument with her folks, she just walked out of their house with bags and baggage.

Shailesh had never expected a move like this from her. "Seema you are most welcome to stay with me." Everything was going on smoothly for a week's time. The landlord of Shailesh's residence objected to Seema staying in with him. He just refused to allow them to stay in his flat. He gave them a month's time to find a new place. "Why do people have to get married to stay together?" said Seema. "Seema our society is not open enough to accept a live-in relationship. If we don't find a new place, we are surely going to fall in trouble. Let's get married." Seema was shocked when she heard this statement. She was in tears. "I am not so bad as you think Seema." Seema said "No Shailesh! I am scared to give our relationship the label of marriage. I feel we will lose the beautiful bond we share. Sometimes I feel people get married only to disagree and fight. Look at my parents married for thirty years but even at this age they are always ready to pounce on each other."

"I am an artist, I try and bring life on my canvas. I have to concentrate a lot when I am painting. If we get married, I will be bowed down by domestic responsibilities."

Seema said "Shailesh I want to be known as a renowned artist. I want to hold exhibitions across the world. I want to hold an exhibition in Paris. I want to visit Europe. I want to see the works of Michael Angelo and Leonardo-da-Vinci."

Shailesh said "Just hold on Seema, I don't have a problem with our relationship. My landlord has just given me a few days and we shall find a new place."

Poor Shailesh took a week's leave for house hunting. He met several estate agents. Most of the people refused to let them their houses as they were in a live-in relationship. Finally, Shailesh found an old bungalow far away from the city. The landlord was an old man who stayed in England. The house had been vacant for a long time. Shailesh had told the estate broker to inform the owners that they were in a live-in relationship. The landlord was just not bothered. He only wanted to let out his house. The house was in a bad condition. It had remained unoccupied for a long time. The only hitch was it was far from the city. Shailesh at once decided to move in the house.

Seema liked the house a lot. "It's so peaceful here, just what I need for my work." "Madam it's ok with you but I will have to drive twenty-five kilometers every day to work." Seema asked Shailesh to give it a second thought if he thought it was so inconvenient. Shailesh decided to go ahead with his decision. None of the housing society flat owners were ready to rent out their houses for a live-in couple. "We have to compromise somewhere."

It took almost a week for Seema and Shailesh to move into their new house. They got the house painted and the garden outside the house was in a very bad state as well. The garden had to be cleaned as well.

Seema was very enthusiastic about the new house. She supervised everything. She made one of the rooms her studio. Shailesh was very surprised to see Seema's new avatar. She brought a new sofa set for their new house. She put two of her paintings in their living room.

Seema converted the rental place into a warm cozy home for Shailesh and her to live in.

Seema managed to get a full-time maid for them and this made things a lot more easier for them.

Shailesh called his parents to see his new place. His parents fussed a lot. After a lot of pleading, they gave in.

Shailesh's mother was very surprised to see the new house. It had a certain sweetness in it. The house had a very homely touch unlike the bachelor pads that Shailesh had occupied in the past.

Shailesh's parents had come to spend only a day or two with them but they were so impressed with Seema's hospitality that they decided to stay back.

Just when Shailesh's mother was leaving to go back home, she called Seema. "Seema you are such a wonderful person. You have changed my opinion about you completely." I think you are made for Shailesh. "Why don't you and Shailesh settle down now? I really fail to understand why you are living like this." Just then Shailesh entered and he heard his mother's words. Shailesh signaled his mother to keep quiet.

His mother continued "Look! Both your father and I are getting old. We want to see you settled."

"Seema, only marriage makes a relationship secure. It's a sacred bond. It's high time you settle down. I don't like it when people point fingers at you." Shailesh's mother's eyes were filled with tears when she left them.

After Shailesh's parents left, Seema was back to her routine again. She was lost in her world of paints and portraits.

Seema was invited to hold an exhibition in one of the art galleries in Paris. Seema was very excited. It was a dream come true. She had decided to give her best this time. Seema decided the theme of her exhibition "Innocence."

Seema made a list of portraits that she wanted to paint. She wished to make portraits of babies, old people with freckled faces and mothers holding babies, young boys and girls. With every portrait she made, she excelled in her craft.

A team from a French magazine had come to interview Seema. Seema was the youngest artist to hold an exhibition in Paris that year. The French team had come with the photographers and journalists. They were very impressed with Seemantini's work. Seema showed them all her paintings and said that she worked solo without anyone's help or interference. One of the journalists asked Seema "How is it possible for you to work for so many hours?" Seema said that she did not have any domestic responsibilities. I am looked after by my partner Shailesh. "I can give my best as I am getting everything on a platter. My life is filled with love where give and take has no role to play." The journalist was stunned to hear this. Seemantini was not only taking her art to another level but she was changing the face of the Indian woman. "Till now we were under the impression that live-in relationships were in only in the west. We believe it has started taking roots in India as well." The journalists left with a lot of photographs and spicy material for their magazine.

A bite of Seema's interview was aired on National TV. Seema didn't expect her interview to be telecast on National TV. Seema's father was the first one to call her after seeing her interview. "Seema what are you up to? Don't forget this that you still carry my name. Seema it was known only locally that I have a shameless daughter who has broken all rules, but now I shall be known throughout the country as the father of bold Seema. Seema, you have been bold enough to walk out of your father's house. Be bold enough and stop using my name. Seema, we are simple people we cannot live like this, where people point fingers at us."

"I think I have been wrong in your upbringing. Seema stop calling yourself Seemantini Pratap Kadam from today. Please, it is an old man's request." Before Seema could give him an explanation, he disconnected the phone. Seema called Shailesh to tell him what her father had said. Shailesh laughed in his usual style. "Seema you are already famous. Famous people create controversies, you have already created one." Seema's voice started quivering. Shailesh could sense that she was crying. "Seema I can't come home just now! Why don't you come to my office? We can have lunch together and then you can go back. This will help you cheer up." Seema agreed at once to do so. People in Shailesh's office were very happy to see Seema. Shailesh's colleagues appreciated Seema's work. His boss asked Seema to give him one of her paintings. Seema agreed to send one of her paintings for him the very next day. Shailesh's office colleagues too joined them for lunch. Seema forgot what her father had said to her at least for the time being.

The same evening when Shailesh came home he was surprised to see Seema sitting quietly with her head buried in her knees. "C'mon Seema you need to pull up your socks. The exhibition is only six months away. You have so much to do." Seemantini started crying bitterly, when she heard Shailesh's words. She embraced him tightly. "Shailesh my world revolves around you. My biological parents have disowned me today. You are my only support in life." Shailesh asked Seema to stop crying first. He wiped her tears "Look Seema, both of us have decided to go against the tide, so it is natural for society to shun us. It's ok as long as we are happy the world does not matter to us. I understand you were very close to your parents. Let's be firm in our stand. Let's wait and see, time is a big healer. I will talk to your father once."

Seema became engrossed in her paintings. She had completed almost fifty paintings. Her only aim now was the exhibition in the art gallery in Paris. Seema's aim was to complete a hundred paintings and that was a huge number.

Seema was not at all feeling well, she was feeling very exhausted, she could not concentrate on her work. This was something unusual and Shailesh too noticed this change in Seema. He asked her to see their family physician. The family physician took a detailed history and asked her to do certain investigations. Seema's reports were normal. The family physician hesitantly asked her if she had missed her periods. Seema said that she had not realized that she had missed her periods. The doctor did a pregnancy test and declared that she was pregnant. Seema left the doctors clinic with a heavy heart. She just couldn't understand what was going on. Why was destiny playing such a joke with her? Seema tried to call Shailesh to tell him this news. All Seema's attempts to contact him turned futile as he was just not reachable.

Seema broke the news to him when he came home that night. Shailesh was shell shocked when he heard the news of Seema's pregnancy. "Oh God No! I don't think you should go ahead with this pregnancy, let's go for an abortion."

Seema shouted "How can you be so heartless? I will never do that. If you don't want to share the responsibility, it's ok. I am strong enough to look after my child." Shailesh said "Seema stop your drama. You are the one who has got this life time opportunity of holding an exhibition in Paris. The pregnancy will be an obstruction in your way. You have not completed a single painting in the last whole week. How are you going to hold an exhibition?"

Seema said "Shailesh, I have decided that I will continue this pregnancy at any cost. I am not going to abort my child. My exhibition can wait. I will get many such chances in the future and even if I don't get a chance like this again, it hardly matters now. My career can wait, I think we should get married as soon as possible. I want our child to be accepted by society. I want to be a responsible mother."

Shailesh could not believe his ears. He said happily "Tomorrow we will get married in a simple ceremony and then we can register our marriage at the marriage registrar's office."

"Shailesh give me a day. I want to buy a new green saree and green bangles. I want to deck up like a bride, your bride." It was time to add a new shade of color to make her life's portrait brighter and better.

Refresher Course

It was about 3:30 pm. Shilpa had just come back from college. She would come back early every Tuesday. Shilpa sat on the plush sofa set of her drawing room. She took hold of her phone and attended to WhatsApp messages. She checked the Facebook as well. There was nothing that amused her. She tried reading, but she started feeling sleepy, the moment she held a book in her hands.

"God! How do my students study?" she thought. "I would definitely fail in these exams." Shilpa used to teach food and nutrition in a home science college. She had a very nice job. Her students admired her. Shilpa literally had a fan following in college. The girls loved her not only for her dressing sense but also for her teaching skills. Shilpa was a good teacher. She taught the girls in such a manner that she made an otherwise boring subject seem interesting.

Shilpa was married to her childhood sweetheart. She had a twelve-year-old daughter Joeta. Shilpa and her husband had grown up together. Two of them were happily married for almost fifteen years now. Everything was going right on all fronts. Shilpa experienced a strange feeling of emptiness. A sense of monotony.

Shilpa was actually leading a very fulfilling life. She never had any financial worries. Her husband was a very understanding person. Her daughter Joeta was an independent and a bright student.

Whenever Shilpa discussed her problems with anyone, they simply laughed at her.

Her colleagues in college always complained of one thing or another, but Shilpa did not complain about anything.

Whenever she talked to Anil, her husband, he never paid much attention to her. "Are we taking each other for granted?" she asked Anil. Anil said "you are simply bored and should do something constructive."

If she pestered him a lot, he would ask her to shop. "Go shopping," he said. Shilpa found this very strange. "Why am I feeling so depressed, so unwanted, so, confused? What's wrong with me?" She even went to a psychiatrist for counseling. "This is midlife crisis," the psychiatrist told her. "Mrs Shilpa Bhave, you have achieved a lot of things at a young age. You have no aims or goals now that is leading to this mental instability syndrome."

Shilpa didn't tell anyone about this.

One day as she entered the staff room, Mrs Pandey, her colleague, showed her a notice issued by the university.

All lecturers and professors had to undergo a refresher course conducted by the university. The staff was asked to visit colleges from the other states so that the government could establish a uniform teaching pattern throughout the country.

Shilpa had to go a university in Gujarat. Shilpa was caught unaware. “Oh God! How do I leave Anil and Joeta?” She didn’t want to avoid this course. The university required her to take the refresher course to qualify as an examiner.

She worried that about the house as she had to leave the city for two weeks. Joeta was too young to control the maids and handle everything. Anil was engrossed in his work. He would not bother to take care of things. Shilpa realized that she was sweating.

Shilpa told Joeta about this course she had to take to qualify as an examiner and her compulsory visit to Gujarat. She expected Joeta to be unhappy to hear that she would not be there for two weeks. Joeta said “yippee… Ma what fun! Daddy and I will go out every day.” Shilpa felt very hurt after seeing Joeta’s reaction but she didn’t show it. She had called Anil to tell him about the refresher course. He didn’t answer her call. He messaged that he was in an important meeting.

The same night when Anil came home, he said “Why were you calling up so desperately yaar, it’s so awkward. I give the phone to my secretary when I am in a meeting and she interrupts me whenever she sees your calls. Now tell me what was so important.” Shilpa said “Anil I have to attend a refresher course in another university for two weeks.” Anil said “So what’s your problem? One has to upgrade one self. This is the need of the hour. Good. You must attend the course, it will do you good and most important it will keep you busy. Shilpa you don't need to see a psychiatrist. If you are busy and your mind is engaged it will keep you away from your restless thoughts."

"Tell me when and where are you going?" Shilpa said "Anil most probably I think I will have to go to either Baroda or Delhi. These are the two colleges that I have to visit."

Anil said "Good, tell me the details so that we can make adjustments at home. I will call my parents and they will come and stay with us. My Aai will take care of the house and so you don't have to worry." Shilpa was mildly annoyed. "Anil how come you have a solution to every problem?" Anil retorted "That's because I think rationally madam." "How come I didn't think of this?" she said to herself.

The next day Shilpa got the details of her refresher course. She was to go away for twelve working days. Shilpa had to go to a women's college in Baroda. She would get accommodation in the college campus. She knew one of the staff from there, Mrs Jyoti Deshpande. She was Shilpa's school friend. She was married and settled in Baroda.

Shilpa was excited that she would get to learn something new and at the same time she was nervous that she had to stay away from Joeta and Anil. She had never left Joeta and stayed away from her. "It's going to be more difficult for me than her." She noticed that Anil too was quite happy that she was going to Baroda. "Shilpa I will tell my peon to do the train bookings. Shilpa, wait a minute, what am I talking? Shilpa, why do you want to travel by train? I will book a flight ticket for you. Find out how far the campus is from the airport?" Shilpa said "Anil you may not recollect but one of my school friends Jyoti Deshpande teaches in the same university that I am going to. Jyoti said that she can pick me up from wherever I stay." "That's fantastic!" exclaimed Anil. "Let me know the dates and I shall book your fight tickets." Shilpa was very happy that Anil took such an interest in how she would travel to Baroda. He was usually not so expressive. After a long time, Shilpa felt very happy and enthusiastic.

The next few days just flew off. Shilpa brought all the required rations for the house. She instructed her maids not to take holidays when she was not there. She shopped a lot for her refresher course. She brought new sarees. She brought a few new *kurtis*. Shilpa talked to her mother-in-law nearly every night. Anil's Aai assured Shilpa that she should not worry. "I will take care of everything." Anil's mother came one day before Shilpa left to Baroda. Aai was not as fit as she used to be. Her knees were weak. She walked with a slight limp. Shilpa felt very guilty to burden her with the responsibilities. Aai was more than happy to come to Pune and stay in her house. Anil dropped Shilpa in the airport. Shilpa's eyes swelled with tears when she said goodbye. Joeta hugged her tightly. "Take care mumma don't worry about us."

Shilpa was traveling alone for the first time. She was feeling a little nervous. Shilpa realized how carefree she would be when she traveled with Anil. Anil usually did all the necessary things. She checked to see whether her check-in luggage tag was there on her purse.

The flight was very comfortable. The man sitting next to her tried to start a conversation with her. Shilpa felt uneasy talking to him. Why do men always take chances when they see a woman alone? Shilpa tried to read the book she was carrying "Not Without My Daughter." He read out the title of the book loudly. "Do you like reading?" Shilpa lost her cool but she didn't want to create a scene. "Look mister, that's none of your business as to what I am reading or doing. Please mind your own business." He was taken aback. He realized that the co-passengers around were looking at him. He pretended to go to sleep.

It was a comfortable journey if only the person next to her had not behaved in a cheap way.

Shilpa was very happy to see Jyoti waiting for her at the airport. Jyoti had changed a lot. She looked older than her age. She had graying in her head but her smile was still the same. Both of them hugged each other. "God, Shilpi you look gorgeous. In fact, you look better, than what you looked in college. Jyoti, it's ages since we have met. Good you have come on a Sunday. You can spend the day at my place and then I shall drop you on the campus." Jyoti took Shilpa home. Jyoti stayed in a joint family. She had two more co-sisters. There were six children in the family. There was a lot of hustle and bustle in the house. Everyone in Jyoti's house was very cordial to her. Shilpa was wondering how Jyoti adjusted with so many people in the house.

Jyoti had made an elaborate lunch for her. When Shilpa praised Jyoti's culinary skills one of the co-sisters passed a nasty remark. "Shilpa if one cooks once in a blue moon, she has to cook well. Look at us, we are constantly cooking or doing household chores, we are not professors!" Jyoti felt uncomfortable. "Come Shilpi, I will show you the house. You have not seen the second floor of our house. I would have asked you to stay with me but you know how it is living in a joint family." Poor Jyoti had tears in her eyes. Shilpa remembered how jovial Jyoti used to be. "How times change."

Just then Jyoti's cell rang. It was Anil calling from Pune. Anil was very annoyed with Shilpa. "Shilpa you have not bothered to call us and tell us you reached safely. See, you have not even bothered to switch your mobile on. I took Jyoti's number from your school friend, Shaheen. I was so worried that you have never been to Baroda before. I was wondering how to contact you. Anyways take care and keep your cell on."

Shilpa felt very ashamed. "How could I be so irresponsible" she said to herself. Jyoti took Shilpa to the Maharaja Sayajirao Gaekwad campus in the evening.

Shilpa was astonished to see the campus. The campus was very beautiful. It had a huge stone building. Jyoti took her around the entire campus. She told her about the famous alumni who had passed out from the Sayajirao Gaekwad University.

Shilpa was allotted a room with an attached toilet. She had to share it with another lecturer who was to come from Mumbai. Shilpa was very pleased with the room. She started unpacking her bags. Jyoti left her and asked her to take care. Jyoti had even packed dinner for Shilpa. Shilpa was very touched by Jyoti's gesture.

Shilpa called home and she spoke at length with Joeta and Anil. Aai complimented Shilpa and said Joeta was a very well-behaved child. "You have groomed your daughter very well Shilpa. I really admire you and even the servants are so well trained. I am really happy to stay here. It is like a holiday for me. Anil's father too should have come along."

Shilpa had her dinner and fell asleep. Early in the morning, she heard loud knocks on her door. Shilpa opened the door. It was her roommate Varsha. She had traveled by road to Baroda. Shilpa helped Varsha to carry her suitcases in the room. They were so heavy. I wonder what she has stuffed inside. Varsha thanked her for helping with the bags. "I am sorry I disturbed you but this was the bus with the cheapest fare, so I opted for it. The auto driver thought I was new. He tried to extract more from me. But I had done my homework. I knew exactly how much it would cost from the bus stand to the campus. I spoke to him in Gujarati. So may be thought I was a localite." Shilpa was very impressed with Varsha. Varsha was younger than Shilpa. Varsha stayed in Mumbai. She had a four-year-old son Vihaan. Varsha showed Shilpa Vihaan's picture on her mobile screen. Slowly Varsha started unpacking her bags. She had bought very few clothes that she hung on the hangers. The other two suitcases were filled with lots of silk and cotton material. Shilpa enquired why she was carrying so much silk and cotton material. "I design and embroider *kurtis* for Khadi Bhandar." "Wow! Is that your hobby?"

Shilpa asked. "It used to be my hobby but now it is my necessity."

Shilpa gave a surprised look to Varsha. She took a long sigh. "What to tell you? How to begin? I got married to Sujay five years back. Mine was an arranged marriage. I don't have a father. I lost my father when I was three or four years old. My poor mother worked very hard to bring me up. I too worked and studied at the same time. I studied and took tuitions while working. I started as a lab assistant. Mrs Bhosale my teacher encouraged me to do postgraduation. Because of her encouragement and backing I completed my postgraduation in textiles and laundry. I joined college immediately as a lecturer. They were the best years of life. I brought a lot of things for my mother and her house. My mother was very keen that I get married and settle down. My mother's maternal uncle brought this proposal. Sujay worked in a firm in the stock exchange. He had a nice flat. His sisters were married. My mother was very happy with the proposal. Our horoscopes matched perfectly. My mother went ahead because of the horoscopes."

Varsha continued "We did the usual business of seeing each other. We met once or twice alone before taking the final decision. My mother was very pleased because Sujay did not make any demands. I too started liking Sujay once I started going out with him. Alas! Little did I know what was in store for me. We got married in a very simple ceremony. I was very happy in my own sweet world. Slowly, slowly I realized Sujay wanted to make it big in a very short time. I tried my best to explain that there is never a short cut to success. He did not pay heed to my advice. He started investing in shares. First two to three times he made a fair amount of profit. This increased his confidence. He started commodity trading. He suffered a huge loss. To overcome this loss, he started gambling. Someone told him about racing. He tried his hand in all sorts of betting, gambling, racing, but everything went futile. Sujay became very aggressive. There was no way we could tide over this financial crisis. I sold whatever little gold I had but that was not enough to keep the creditors away."

"I took a personal loan to pay all of his loans. I mortgaged my house. My entire salary was spent on paying the EMIs for the personal loans that I have taken. Sujay is not doing anything now. He is into depression. He tried committing suicide. I had to keep him in a rehabilitation center. He is not himself at all."

"I design *kurtis* and embroider sarees for Khadi Bhandar. They pay me well. With this money, I manage my household expenses. Sujay's parents have disowned us. They feel I am responsible for his downfall. They blame me that I could not control him. I have decided, however, hard I have to work I am going to treat him and bring him back to normal. I don't want my Vihu to grow up without a father. Sometimes I break down and I ask God why me? But then I remember how boldly my mother raised me single handedly. I will be a coward if I run away or do anything wrong. Now I understand the motto of our SNDT College 'Enlightened Women is a Source of Infinite Strength.' I keep saying this to myself. I say this when God closed one door he has opened another door."

"Just when I needed, the Khadi Bhandar people approached me to design their *kurtis*. It's a very well-known and old store in Mumbai. They pay me well enough to run my house well and take treatment for Sujay. My mother helps me out in her own way. She is a great asset. She looks after my son, she looks after Sujay. Aai takes him to the doctor whenever needed. She is the one who gives Sujay all the medicines in time. Aai is very confident, she always says that if you are educated, if you are independent, then you will definitely tide over the crisis." Shilpa had tears in her eyes. She embraced Varsha after hearing her story. "You are indeed a brave woman. Varsha you are a super achiever in my eyes. You need to be applauded for the courage and understanding you are showing." Varsha said "No Shilpa, there are times when I break down." Shilpa felt very ashamed of herself. "I am actually like a queen, and still I crib for small things." Shilpa asked Varsha to freshen up. She made tea for both of them. Shilpa had brought instant tea packets with her. "This tea is so refreshing, thank you this is what I needed." Shilpa remembered what a comfortable flight she had. "Varsha will you teach me how you design and embroider so that I can help you." Varsha was more than happy to hear this from Shilpa. "Can I call you Tai please?" she asked. Varsha said "Of course, you can." Varsha excused herself. She had to call home and inform Sujay and Aai that she had reached safely. Nobody answered her phone. "Aai must be busy getting things done for Vihu and Sujay is not in a state to understand anything. Shilpa Tai he just keeps on staring. If I ask him anything he doesn't respond." Shilpa said "It's ok, times will change."

Shilpa called home. Anil was very happy to speak to her. "Is your room comfortable? If you are not happy, you can move into a hotel. Don't bother about the expenses. Comfort is important." Shilpa said "No Anil, the room is OK but I have found a new friend Varsha. She is a lecturer from Mumbai. She has proved to be an eye opener. When I come back from the refresher course you will notice a great change in me." Anil said "Hold on! Hold on! Shilpa I am getting nervous, tell me what are you thinking now. Remember, I love you very much and we need you very much." Shilpa shivered when she heard this. "Anil, I too love both of you very much, thank you for being so nice, so supportive, so caring, so..."

Break Up

Shaila was at the cash counter in the bank. She was concentrating on her work. Monday mornings were really difficult. Everybody was in a hurry to get their cash transactions done.

Her mobile rang. It was her maid Shanta. "Madam please come home. Bhavna has come home from college. She has locked herself in her room. She is crying endlessly. Bhavna baby is not opening the door." Shaila remembered Sapna her younger daughter was at home. "Bai, ask Sapna to talk to her." Shantha said "Both of us have been trying to make Bhavna to open the door. She is just not responding." Sapna snatched the phone from the maid's hand. "Mumma, come home. Sister is just not listening."

Shaila was shocked to hear about Bhavna's strange behavior. Bhavna had never thrown any tantrums before. Shaila left her counter. She requested the manager to grant her leave. "How can you go Mrs Gaikwad?" he said. Shaila had to literally beg him to grant her leave. "Sir, my daughter is not well? I need to go." Finally, Shaila's boss gave in. Shaila left her office in a hurry. She caught an auto. The ten-minute ride seemed like an endless journey. Her thoughts were running like horses. Why was Bhavna behaving like this? She came back to normal when the auto driver told her that she had reached her destination.

"Madam, why are you looking so worried?" he enquired. After all, all auto drivers are not so bad. Sapna and Shanta were still thumping their fists on the door. "Open the door Bhavna. Tell me what is wrong? Have you failed in your exams?" Sapna turned towards her mother and said "Mummy, sister does not have any exams now. She is wasting my time. I have board exams next month." Shaila asked Sapna to keep quiet.

Shaila continued "Bhavna, please listen. Listen to your mommy." Finally, Bhavna opened the door. She embraced her mother and started crying. Shaila asked the maid to go out. "Darling, tell me what is wrong."

Bhavna finally said "Mumma, Ravi and I broke up today."

Shaila asked shocked "Why? What happened? What went wrong? Last week you went out for a movie." "I knew this" Sapna intervened. "I never liked Ravi." "Sapna just get out." Bhavna shouted back at her. Sapna left the room by banging the door.

"It's ok, stop crying. I will talk to him." Bhavna said "No mumma. It's over, he was behaving very rudely. I asked him why he was behaving like this. He just started shouting. It was so awkward. He said he was sick of me. He said he was fed up of answering my questions. He also said 'Don't ever talk to me, I don't want to see your face ever again.' That's what he said, mumma. He said all this in the library on top of his voice." Shaila said soothingly

"You stop crying first Bhavna. Then we will analyze what went wrong. He may have been tensed as he is in the final year. May be the stress of studies is taking a toll on him." Bhavna said "No mumma. I can't believe this, it is the same Ravi who followed me for a month till I said yes to him."

Shaila said "Go wash your face, let's eat something." Bhavna said "No mumma. I don't feel like eating." Bhavna refused to eat anything that day. Shaila called her husband Shri to tell him what had happened. He asked Shaila to stay with Bhavna. The same evening when Shri came home, he was devastated to see Bhavna. "What has that fool done to my girl? Shaila give me his number." Shaila tried to control Shri's rage. "Look Shri, we need to deal with the situation in a very mature manner." Shri shouted "This is no way to behave, wait till I get hold of that..."

Shaila said "Shri you were the one with a progressive attitude you gave the girls a lot of freedom. I had warned you several times."

Shri angrily said "Shut up Shaila. I don't want your sermons now." Shaila said firmly "Look Shri, we need to forget our differences and concentrate on Bhavna."

Shri calmed down and said "Shaila, first time in my life I am feeling so helpless. I can't bear to see my Bhavna crying so much. She is hurt."

Shaila brought him a cup of tea. Shri continued "That ...is not worthy of my girl, such an intelligent, beautiful girl."

Shri was extremely proud of his daughters. Shri had never imagined that they would have to experience something like this.

Shri stormed into Bhavna's room. "Look, you are not going to patch up with that fool. He doesn't deserve you. A person who cannot respect you is not worthy of you." Shaila was taken aback to hear these words from Shri.

Shaila said "We need to give her some time." Shri said "This generation makes relationships easily. That's why they break up also easily. Bhavna stop being an emotional fool. Don't think about him again."

Shaila realized that she was still in her office clothes. She had a splitting headache. Whom should I tell what I am going through?

Shri made himself a peg of whisky and settled in front of the TV. Bhavna was curled up in her bed. She was staring blankly at the ceiling. Shaila hugged her daughter tightly. "Bhavna, in a way it is a blessing in disguise. It is better to break up than carry on with a person you can't get along with." Bhavna turned and looked at her mother. "But mumma, I never had a problem with him. It was Ravi who broke up with me. Mumma! He wants to concentrate on his studies. Can you believe this mumma? I always helped him. I did his submissions. I wrote notes for him. He would go to play football and I like a fool would sit and complete his submissions." Just then, Bhavna's friend Pooja came in. "Hi aunty! Bhavna, why are you not answering your phone? You just left college without informing me." Shaila went to bring something to eat for Pooja. "My mom and dad know about the showdown."

Pooja said "Bhavna I know it's painful." She had been a witness to the entire affair right from day one. Shaila entered the room. "Let's not talk about it," said Bhavna. Shaila said "Pooja, tell Bhavna what she missed in college today." Pooja said "What aunty says is right Bhavna. Just behave like nothing has happened. After you left, I gave Ravi a piece of my mind." Shaila said "Pooja, you need to take care of Bhavna. After all you are her best friend."

The same night Shaila slept with Bhavna. Bhavna did not sleep a wink. She tossed and turned in her bed. "Mumma, why did he do this?" Shaila, did not have an answer to this.

Next morning, everybody was busy in their own routine. Sapna was studying her chemistry equations. Shri was reading the newspaper. Shaila was organizing the breakfast and lunch with Shanta.

"Shaila, it's eight. Why is Bhavna not getting ready for college?" Shri asked Shaila to go and see what Bhavna was doing. "Mumma, please, I don't want to go to college today. I have a terrible headache." Shaila's heart melted for her girl. "Shri, she is complaining of headache." Shri said "Let her have breakfast, give her medicine, if she feels alright, let her go to college. Otherwise, ask her rest at home today."

Shaila had an important meeting in the bank today. She could not afford to stay back at home. "Sapna, Bhavna is not feeling well. Just look after her." Sapna said

"Mumma, now she is overacting why can't she get over that dumbo."

"Shut up Sapna, how mean can you be." Shaila was very upset with Sapna's attitude. "Shanta look after Bhavna. She is not feeling well." The maid assured Shaila that she would stay with Bhavna till she came back from office. Shaila was very touched with the maid's words. She pushed a hundred rupee note in Shanta's hand. "What would I have done without Shanta?"

Shaila was restless in office. She called home to find out what Bhavna was doing.

Shri and Shaila decided to talk to Ravi's parents. They were also aware of Bhavna and Ravi's affair. Shaila dialed Mrs Deshpande's number. "Hello Mrs Deshpande? How are you? I need to talk to you. I know what you are going to say." Ravi's mother said "Look Mrs Gaikwad. Ravi is our only son. We have lot of plans for him. Bhavna was proving to be a hindrance in his way." Ravi's mother's words shocked Shaila. "What are you talking? My Bhavna tamed your boy. She was the one who taught him to be sincere in his work. Bhavna helped him in his studies. She completed his submissions. His scores improved after he started dating Bhavna. Mrs Deshpande why don't you make Ravi understand. See everyone has differences but you can't ditch someone after three years. Come and see Bhavna's state. The poor girl is shattered." Ravi's mother said "Mrs Gaikwad thank your stars, my boy was decent, he could have taken undue advantage of your girl. He has never crossed his limits. What if he feels like moving out of a relationship? It is better to break up than carry on."

It was useless talking to this lady. Shri was shocked when he heard Mrs Deshpande's words. "Shaila shake that girl and tell her to forget that fool. We have to teach her to move on."

Bhavna was still in the mourning phase. She was mourning for the love she had lost. Bhavna didn't attend college for almost a week. "Shaila you need to put some sense into Bhavna." Shaila was finding it very difficult to deal with Shri and Bhavna at the same time.

Shaila lost her patience once day. "Look Bhavna enough is enough. I understand what you are going through. But don't ruin your career. Your dad and I are paying a lot for your education. You know what all we did to secure a seat in this private engineering college. Just concentrate on your studies. I will say it was the other way round. The boy was proving to be a distraction. Look Sapna too is getting disturbed. She has to appear for her board exams next month. Your papa is so disturbed."

Bhavna did not pay attention to what Shaila said. She thought about what Ravi had said. She just couldn't accept the fact that Ravi had broken up with her. What happened to the promises? What happened to the plans! She remembered how she would joke with Ravi. "I missed my government college seat just by one mark, because I was destined to meet you here." Bhavna brushed aside her thoughts.

The next day, Bhavna got up earlier than usual. She checked out the lectures that were scheduled for that day. Pooja was very happy that finally Bhavna was coming to college. Pooja missed hanging around with Bhavna in college. Shri and Shaila were very happy that Bhavna had finally gathered the confidence to attend college.

Bhavna reached the college gate. She just didn't have the guts to get in. She turned from the gate, but then thought that if she did not attend college that day, then her mother and father would be upset. Bhavna drove past her college on her Scooty. She had no idea where she was heading. She went so far that she lost her way. Just imagine losing your way to reach your own house. She had to ask people the way back home.

This went on for three or four days. One day, she spent the entire day on a bench in a park. Some boys started passing nasty comments at her so she had to run from there. "A temple is a safe place" she thought. She went all the way to Sarasbaug. She thought she would find solace in the serenity of the temple. However, she did not find peace anywhere.

Pooja called Bhavna every day and Bhavna always responded that she would attend college the next day, but she never did. Finally, Pooja complained to Bhavna's parents that Bhavna had stopped attending college. Shri was also there when Pooja came home. "Aunty, Bhavna is not attending college." When Shri heard this he barged into Bhavna's room. "Bhavna did you attend college today?" Bhavna said "Yes, Pappa." When Shri heard this he was so furious that he slapped Bhavna. Shaila heard the noise and rushed in. Shri had never done this before and Pooja was taken aback. She had never expected something like this to happen. Shaila asked Shri to leave the room. "Why did you lie to us Bhavna?" Bhavna explained

"Mumma, I just don't understand what is going on. I don't have the courage to go to college? What will people say?" Her mother scolded Bhavna. "Bhavna, how can you be so selfish? You are crying for a person who doesn't care a damn for you.

Don't we have any place in your life. Your Pappa and me keep on worrying about you. Have you ever realized what pains we have taken to raise you up?" Pooja too started crying. Shaila hugged Pooja, "Don't worry, everything will be fine."

Pooja said "I stay far aunty. Otherwise, I would have come every day to take Bhavna to college." Shaila said "Go home Pooja, it's getting late and don't forget to call me when you reach home." Shri came to Bhavna's room. "I didn't mean to insult you and that too in front of your friend. You have never hidden anything from us. You were bold enough to tell us about Ravi. We have been lenient with you. It hurts me to see you like this." Shri had tears in his eyes. Shaila had never seen Shri like this before. Shaila too started crying.

The same night before going to sleep, Shaila invited Shri to the drawing room. "I need to talk to you Shri. It is almost three weeks now, since Bhavna and Ravi broke up. I feel Bhavna can't cope with this stress. She needs counseling. She is going into depression. Shri we need to bring our girl back to normal." Shri was very furious when he heard this. "Have you lost it Shaila? Are you really Bhavna's mother? How can you take her to a psychiatrist? Do you want her to be labeled as a mad person? People will start talking about this. Now very few people know about her affair. If you take her to a psychiatrist and if this leaks out we will be in trouble."

Her mother said "Shri, please think rationally. If we don't treat her now, we will land in great trouble. What if she leaves her education half way? What if she develops suicidal tendencies? Shri, what will we do?"

Shri said "Shaila, I have lost my ability to think." Shaila said "C'mon Shri. How can you lose hope? We have to overcome this crisis. Shri I have taken an appointment with the psychiatrist tomorrow. Let us go and meet him."

Shri and Shaila spent the whole night pacing up and down. Shaila tried to put on a brave front but she too was unable to decide whether what she was doing was right.

The next evening, Shaila went to the psychiatrist clinic. She was surprised to see so many patients in his waiting room. Do people suffer from so many mental illnesses? Finally, Shaila's turn came. She told the doctor everything about Bhavna's behavior. The doctor advised "These are early signs of depression. The girl is very sensitive and the break up has not been digested by her. Bring her tomorrow." Shaila took great care when she was stepping out of Dr D'souza's clinic. She didn't want anyone to spot her.

Next day, she took Bhavna to Dr D'souza's clinic. He listened very carefully to whatever Bhavna said. He prescribed some antidepressants and multivitamins for her. He asked Shaila and Bhavna to see him after fifteen days. There was a marked improvement in Bhavna's behavior. She stopped being restless. "Mumma, will you accompany me to college. Please,..." Shaila was touched by Bhavna's request. How could anyone have the heart to break such a sensitive girl's heart.

"Yes, I will accompany you." Shaila would accompany Bhavna till the college gate. Pooja would then take over from her. Shaila would wait outside Bhavna's college. Slowly, Bhavna started getting back to normal.

Dr D'souza's medicines and counseling brought a lot of change in Bhavna.

God knows from where Mrs Deshpande spotted Shaila and Bhavna coming out of Dr D'souza's clinic. Mrs Deshpande had the audacity to go to Shaila and ask her who needed the psychiatrist's help. "We are done Mrs Deshpande, but soon you may need the doctor's help since your son doesn't understand human values and the importance of love. Don't be surprised if he ditches you also." Mrs Deshpande hung her face down and walked away.

Reparation

Mita had a very hectic schedule. She lived in the suburbs and her office was in South Mumbai. Mita worked as a senior maintenance officer for a reputed firm. Her firm sold air conditioners. Mita looked after their maintenance contracts. She was working for more than fifteen years. At times Mita would think of quitting the job, but then she would think of EMIs that she and Vinod, her husband, were paying, she would drive away these thoughts. "Luxuries always come with a price."

Mita and Vinod lived in a three bedroom flat in one of the elite societies. Vinod had always wanted the best for his children. Mita always wondered why Vinod never compromised in life. Mita kept up with the rat race to support Vinod in fulfilling his aims and ambitions. Mita would get up early in the morning and with the maids help she would get the kids ready for school; she would pack their lunch boxes. Mita would instruct the maids to carry out the other household chores for the day before she left for office.

Vinod would drop Mita at the local train station every day in his car. Mita would be on her feet the entire day. Mita would meet all the important clients: she would sign the maintenance contracts for the air conditioners that her company sold. Mita would work till 5 pm. She would catch either the 5.30 or 6'o clock fast local train to reach home.

Mita would meet with a nice group of friends including her college friends Smita and Sandira while going back home in the local train. The local train journey was her only relaxation in the day. At home, she would help Bacchu and Chakuli with their homework. Vinod would come home later and they would have dinner together. The children would go to sleep. After dinner, Vinod would surf through the TV channels and the TV remote would always be in his control. Mita would always think how Vinod could tolerate Arnab's show. When Vinod would be tired of surfing through the channels, he would divert his attention towards Mita. Later, Mita would have to perform her duties as a wife and most of the times unwillingly. Everything was mechanical and the passion was lacking. In early days, Mita would long to meet Vinod. "How times change" she thought. Sometimes she would feel that she was living with a stranger. "How could I fall head over heels in love with this man?" Mita always found Vinod very mature and caring. Mita had quite a few admirers in college. She had a fling or two in the past, but...Vinod was the love of her life. Vinod was a self-made man. He came from a rural background and he had no support from his family. Vinod had achieved a lot in the past decade. He had bought a decent house and they had a four wheeler. Their house was very well furnished. They had hired a well-known interior designer. Their house had all the modern gadgets. Mita would feel lost in this sea of amenities.

Vinod would pamper the children a lot and the children would be all over him. Mita would often complain about this to Vinod. "I work from morning to night too for these rascals and the moment they see you they ditch me. It is hard to earn their respect. I never thought children are calculative."

Vinod traveled a lot. Mita would manage everything alone. She would look after Bacchu and Chakuli. When Chakuli would cry for Vinod, she would get very irritated. She would spank Chakuli for her behavior. But Chakuli would become more adamant. When, Mita discussed this with her mother, her mother said that she too did the same when Mita was young. Whenever Mita brought up the topic of Vinod's indifference, Mita's mother hushed her up. Mita's mother would pacify Mita, "He is bogged down, by his work tensions." Mita would argue "What about me? Aai, I am also a working woman, I don't behave like him." Her mother would say "nature has made women more understanding and supportive." Lately, Mita had stopped discussing her problems with her Aai. She felt her mother was biased towards Vinod.

One day, Vinod said "Mita I have to leave for Nagpur tonight. I have an evening flight. I will leave directly from office. I need your help to pack my bag." Mita said "There is an open day tomorrow in our children's school. Vinod, I thought you will be attending it. How can you back out at the eleventh hour?" Vinod argued "C'mon Mita I am not doing things intentionally. Don't blow things out of proportion." Mita was very upset with Vinod. He immediately mellowed, "Let Bacchu and Chakuli's teachers know what a smart mother they have."

Vinod would always flatter her when he wanted Mita to do something for him or the children. Vinod sensed that Mita was angry so packed his bag on his own. Vinod called out to Bacchu and Chakuli. "I am going on a tour. I won't be there for your open day. Your mummy will be there, don't you dare trouble her." Mita didn't speak a word to Vinod when he came to drop her at the station.

Mita was very quiet on the local train journey that day. Her friends asked her the reason for her silence and when Mita told them the reason, everybody had a different opinion. "You should make the best of this situation. It's your bonding time with the kids. Take the kids out and enjoy." This was Sandira's advice to Mita.

Later that day Mita was going through her files in the office when the peon told her that the boss had called her to his cabin. "Mita we have a new recruit joining us tomorrow. He is our MD Mr Khurana's nephew. I give this duty of looking after him to you. Explain our work to him. Give him our VIP client list. Tell him about our maintenance agreements." Mita tried hard to concentrate on Mr Singh's instructions. Finally, she gathered the courage to interrupt him. "Sir, I want leave tomorrow, only for one day sir, please excuse me. I have to attend the open day in my children's school. It's compulsory to attend the open day, my husband is out of station. Sir, these convent schools are very strict." Mr Singh gave in to Mita's requests.

"Ok Mita you can take leave for one day. But... explain everything to him and see that everyone behaves well with him." Mita sighed in relief and reached her cabin. When Mita reached home she remembered that she had forgotten to instruct the maid about the evening dinner. The maid had taken the liberty of cooking what she wanted. Mita thanked her stars that Vinod was not there. The kids refused to eat the vegetables that the *bai* had made. Mita decided to order something from the restaurant close by. Chakuli was already scrubbing her eyes. Bacchu gave her the bright idea of making pasta. Just like the moms in the advertisements on TV she made pasta in a few minutes. All three of them enjoyed their dinner.

The open day was a great success. Both Bacchu and Chakuli had done very well in their unit tests. The teachers praised the children a lot. "Homework always complete on time. They are neat and tidy all the time. They are well-behaved children." Mita felt pleased when she heard these praises. After all, she was their mother. Mita was happy that Vinod was not there. He would have boasted how much he had taken care of the children. Mita took the children out for lunch. All three of them had a nice day out.

In the evening, Mita accompanied the children to the children's park in the society. "Oh! My God! Mrs Mane. Are you Bacchu's and Chakuli's mother? We never see you! You must mingle with your neighbors." Mita just smiled. "I reach home at six-thirty. Where do I have the time to sit idle?" "You must find time" said Mrs Banerjee their neighbor. "When will Dadda come?" asked Chakuli. Mita pulled her close and made her sit on her lap. She signaled Bacchu also to come close. Of late, Bacchu showed a lot of attitude. He tried to stay away from the hugs and kisses. After all, he was going to be twelve now. The next morning, Mita had just entered the office when she saw a young man coming towards her table. "Oh! So this is the new recruit."

"Good morning madam. I am Akash Khurana." She thought that the name was from a movie. "Mr Singh has asked me to take orders from you." She said "Let me correct you. I am supposed to help you and not order you. Mr Akash you work with me for some time, once you understand our functioning you can work from your desk." Mita found Akash to be very smart and net savvy. In fact, he showed her newer and easier ways of storing client data.

One day he said "Madam, can I ask you a personal question? Are you married?"

"Married!" exclaimed Mita. "I am a mother of two children. My son is twelve and my daughter is seven." "What! What are you saying?" He said "You look so young Mita madam." Mita felt very happy to receive this compliment. Mita said "Let's get back to work." Mita explained everything to Akash. She gave him their VIP client lists. She showed him the details of their maintenance records. Akash grasped whatever Mita said very quickly. At lunch time, Mita introduced Akash to the entire staff. Akash mingled with them very well. As they returned to their respective places Akash whispered in Mita's ears. "You are the sweetest person in the office."

Mita was taken aback. "What is this man up to?" Akash would always find reasons to talk to her. Finally, Mita lost her cool one day. "Mr Akash, I am a mother of two and I have a reputation to live up to. You better understand this." Akash banged his fists on Mita's table and said, "That's what I am trying to tell you Mrs Mita Mane. Why are you so aloof? We live life only once, all of us have the right to enjoy. Why can't the work-place be a fun place? Open up Mita, stop being so serious."

Just then Mrs Ayushi Joshi, another colleague, intervened. "I feel what Akash says is right, this office is suffocating." Akash said "Let's go for a picnic this weekend. How about Lonavala?" Everybody in the office agreed at once. "We will have to ask Mr Singh for permission." The next day, the entire office staff asked Mr Singh about going to Lonavala for a picnic. Mr Singh agreed at once. He asked their permission to bring his wife to the picnic. Mita also agreed. She had to. Even the peons were to accompany them. After all, they were one big happy family. Everybody looked forward to the office picnic. Finally, the day of the picnic arrived. Everybody was in high spirits. Mr and Mrs Singh too joined the staff in the merriment. Mr Singh enthralled everyone with his songs. Nobody knew that Mr Amardeep Singh was such a jovial person. He amused everyone with his jokes. Mrs Ayushi Joshi organized games for the staff. Akash came up with the bright idea of playing cricket. There was fun and *masti*. Everybody was very tired by the time they reached V.T. Station.

Mita told Vinod about the day out. How much she had enjoyed herself. "I thought you had forgotten to smile Mita" said Vinod. Mita got irritated and wanted to smack him for this statement.

The Sunday that followed the picnic just flew away. Sunday was not a holiday. It was a working day at home.

The entire office staff was in high spirits on Monday morning. Mr Amardeep Singh thanked Akash for organizing such a good picnic. Everybody cheered for Akash. At lunchtime, Mrs Fernandes complained how she had to pack lunch for herself and her kids. "There is no break from this" she said. Akash said that one day in a week all of them should not bring lunch from home. "We will order something from the nearby restaurants. The ladies will be saved of the trouble of packing lunch for at least one day." "It will be fun" everyone echoed in union.

"God knows from where he comes with such bright ideas." The entire office staff was very happy. There was a lot of teasing and joking in the office. Mita too joined the staff in the fun-n-frolic. She actually played cards with them during lunch time. The staff performances improved. The reason for this was the relaxed atmosphere in the office. People concentrated more when they were working. Everybody wanted to finish their work and enjoy.

Mita didn't realize how friendly she had become with Akash. He asked Mita out for lunch. Mita agreed at once without any inhibitions. He took her to one of the posh restaurants. Akash had booked a table for two. He ordered all her favorite chicken dishes. Mita asked Akash "How do you know my preferences?" He replied "I can read people like a book. Mita you have a beautiful smile, keep on smiling." Mita said "Please don't flatter me Akash." He said "I am serious Mita. You are not only beautiful, but you are intelligent as well. This is a rare combination." Mita said "Enough lets go back." Just as they entered the office, Ms. Ayushi chided "Akash. Take me also out for lunch sometime." Akash immediately fell down on his knees and held Mrs Joshi's hand. "Anytime young lady, the pleasure is mine." Mrs Ayushi Joshi was taken aback. She had never expected Akash to react this way.

The lunches and the card games continued. Akash was like the Pied Piper of Hamlyn. Everyone just followed him.

Mita just didn't realize when she fell in love with him. "If only I had met you a few years back, my life would have been so different." "Yeah! You would have been a mother of a dozen children instead of two" said Akash. "This is what I like about you" said Mita. "You are so carefree; you are just not bothered about the world." This office affair went on almost for a year. One fine day, Mita finally gathered the courage to talk to Akash. "I want to talk to you Akash." "Anytime sweetheart, I am at your service" he said. "Not here in office, let's get out first." Mita and Akash left the office early under some pretense.

"Akash! I feel very guilty. I am leading a dual life. I go home, I am a different person. I come to office, I am a different person. I can't bear this hypocrisy. I think it's high time, I told Vinod about our relationship. I will tell him I want a divorce. Vinod is very attached to the children and he will take care of them. I want to start a new life with you."

"Hold on! Hold on Mita! Do you understand what you are talking about? Have you lost it? I just meant friendship. You mistook me. I don't like commitments. We met as friends, we enjoyed as friends. I enjoy your company but I don't want any strings attached. You can leave your husband and family. You can come and live with me but don't ask for marriage. I don't believe in commitments. When there are commitments, there are expectations. When there are expectations, there is always unhappiness." Mita started crying inconsolably. "Don't create a scene Mita, people are watching us." Mita couldn't believe what she had heard. Mita left the restaurant in a hurry. She caught a taxi to go back home.

"How could I betray Vinod for a person like Akash?" she thought. She felt ashamed. When she reached home, Chakuli noticed her tear-stained face and asked "Are you not well mumma? Mumma lie down, I will press your head." Bacchu got her a glass of water and a pain- killer. Mita was very touched by the children's gestures. She cried more profusely. The maid gave her a cup of tea. "Sleep for some time, you will feel better and don't bother about the children. I will wait till Vinod *sahib* comes home. Madam, I will serve him dinner and then leave." Even the maid showed so much concern.

Bacchu had called up Vinod to tell him that Mita was not well. When Vinod came home, he touched Mita's forehead to see whether she had fever. "Should I make coffee for you Mita? Mita, you look very tired. Why don't you take leave for a few days? You have so many casual leaves pending. I will call your mother. She can stay with us and look after you." The moment Mita heard this, she thought "How selfish I have been, I have not seen Aai for the last three months." Mita cried again. Vinod held her close, "Why are you crying so much Mita? Don't tell me you can't bear a simple headache." Vinod pressed her forehead. He did this till she fell asleep.

Mita's mother arrived at seven the next morning. She caught the first local train so that she could see Mita as soon as possible "*Kay zhale Mita.*" Mita was touched by her mother's words. "I am seeing you after such a long time, look at yourself, just skin and bones. You should take care of yourself. Vinod, why are you not strict with her. Is this girl eating? I bet she is working a lot. Work in the office, work at home. This had to happen someday. Mita lie down, now that I have come I will manage everything."

Aai got the children ready. She made "Thalipeeth" for Vinod's breakfast. Vinod relished Mita's mother's food.

"Why don't you stay with us mother-in-law?" asked Vinod.

"*Nahi re Baba*, who will look after my old man? He can't do anything on his own. Mita is unwell, so he sent me. That reminds me, I have to remind him to take his insulin with his breakfast."

Mita's mother was a battered wife. Mita's father used to abuse his wife and that too for no reason. Her Aai was so tolerant.

Vinod said "Mita I have taken Dr Gandhi's appointment at 11 am. Go and see him. Aai you accompany Mita to the doctor. Mita take rest. Don't start cleaning once you feel better." Aai brought breakfast for Mita. "Eat this; it will make you feel better. Mita if you rest and eat well you will be fine. Mita, remember you are a human being and not a machine. You can't work continuously. You have not visited us in the past two to three months. Whenever I called you, you were in a hurry. Mita don't work beyond your limits."

"Aai please sit next to me. I am sorry I went wrong" said Mita. Her mother said "It's alright dear but take care of your health. I cannot leave your father. His sugar fluctuates, his blood pressure (BP) shoots up. Ashwini has brought him an automatic BP apparatus." Ashwini was Mita's sister-in-law. "Ashwini is a nice girl and she cares a lot for us. She is no different from you. She works in the office every day and when she is at home she looks after Rohan. He troubles her lot. He doesn't see his mother the whole day. It is natural for children to trouble their mothers a lot."

Mita asked "Aai how did you tolerate baba?" Her mother responded "I had no alternative. Where could I have gone if I left him? I only thought about you and your brother."

Mita said "Aai, I want to confess something." Her mother asked "Is Vinod troubling you?" Mita said "No. Aai? I have gone wrong. I was infatuated. There is a guy called Akash. He joined our office last year. I don't know how, but I got involved with him." Mita's mother was shocked to hear this. Mita's mother closed the room door. She didn't even want the maid to listen to their conversation.

"Aai this mundane routine was taking a toll on me. He came like a magician and he enthralled me with his sweet talks. I decided to settle with him and start a new life with him." Her mother said "Mita, are you mad? Have you lost your senses? Didn't you think about your children? Look at your husband. The poor guy works from morning to night so that you can live comfortably. Mita, you are my daughter. You have seen me suffer at the hands of your father. My only fault was that I was beautiful and I was an orphan. Your father felt that he owned me. He always doubted my character. I would work hard throughout the month and the day I would get my salary, he would snatch away my salary. I had to beg him for my own money. I was not educated enough to understand my rights. I traveled in the third class compartment in the local trains. I had only two sarees to wear. We never had any servants or any help whatsoever. Do you remember our old house in the *chawl*? There were many people who tried to be friendly, but I never fell prey to anything."

"Mita, every person has a right to be happy. But you cannot be happy by making others unhappy. I sent you to an English medium school. I tried my best to give you all the things that I had missed. Mita, what use is your education if you cannot differentiate between good and bad? Is that fellow younger than you?" Mita just nodded her head. "How could you fall prey to a young fellow's tricks? Thank your stars. You realized your mistake before it was too late. Does Vinod know anything about this?" Mita responded dejectedly "No Aai, he doesn't have the slightest idea, but I am going to tell him everything. I will be at peace only if I tell him the truth." Mita's mother vigorously nodded her head no. "Are you crazy girl!

There is no need to do so. What if Vinod gets offended? We are humans and not Gods! There is nothing wrong in going wrong, but you need to correct yourself. I will not allow you to do anything stupid now. It is over now. You need to start life again. Just forget everything and begin life like nothing had happened."

Her mother said "Let me deal with the situation." Vinod called from his office to find out what Dr Gandhi had said. They were supposed to have gone to see Dr Gandhi. Mita's mother answered the phone. Mita was fast asleep, so she didn't wake Mita. Her mother spoke to Vinod. "She is much better now, her headache has also decreased." Mita woke up just then and was surprised at her mother's presence of mind. The old lady was taking care of the situation. Dr Gandhi would have advised Mita to take a number of tests. Mita's mother and Mita knew the reason for Mita's ill health.

Mita's mother said "Mita, get up and freshen up. It's time for the children to come home. Why don't you make something for them to eat? It will divert our attention."

The same evening Vinod came back from work and enquired how Mita was. "She is tired because of overwork" her mother said. Vinod said "She works from six in the morning till nine in the night. I have told her a thousand times not to work so hard. I am ready to leave her to the office in my car, but no, Madam wants to travel by local train." Mita responded "I get to meet my friends." Vinod demanded "Are friends so important?" He then looked at Mita's mother and said "We have two maids to help her but no, she is constantly doing something or the other.

Forever cleaning. She has obsessive compulsive disorder." "What's that?" asked Mita's mother. Vinod said "She can't tolerate uncleanliness. These children also trouble her a lot."

"That's the reason she got carried away" Mita's mother bit her tongue. Fortunately, Vinod did not hear her.

"It has been ages since both of us have taken a vacation. There is a nice package. Three nights and four days in a five star hotel in Goa. If you stay back and look after the children. I can take Mita to Goa." This was a huge surprise to Mita. Vinod was suddenly in a holiday mood. Had he sensed something? Was he trying to make up for something he had done?

BALANCE–IMBALANCE

Sujata and Shreya watched as Jaydeep packed his bags. Sujata tried hard to control her tears. She didn't want to cry in front of him, at least not today.

Sujata hurried to the kitchen under the pretense of making coffee. Sujata thought "Why am I lamenting over a dead relationship? Is it because of the number of years we have spent together?"

She could not control her tears that were flowing down her cheeks. "Thank you so much for the coffee. This was just what I needed." Jaydeep settled on the sofa in his usual place and had his coffee.

Sujata sipped her coffee. "You sat on this sofa and ruled over me" she said to herself. So finally the day had come and Jaydeep was moving out of their house. Jaydeep was surprised to see the number of things he had packed. He realized that he had made a big mess. "Sorry Sujata, you are going to curse me a hundred times when you start cleaning the mess I have created." Sujata felt like shaking him up and saying "You have already messed up my life. What more can you do to trouble me?"

Jaydeep sat close to his daughter and hugged her and kissed her. "Shreya, if you need anything just call me. I am just a phone call away. Don't hesitate to ask me for anything. You are and you will always be my princess. I will come and meet you every weekend." He turned towards Sujata and said "take care." Without looking at her, he picked up his bags and walked out.

Jaydeep too felt very uneasy. There was heaviness in his chest after he said his final goodbye. Sujata thought "Take care... my foot. If you were so concerned, you wouldn't have left us." Jaydeep and Sujata were divorced. All the love and all the sweet memories of wonderful years they had spent together were destroyed with just two signatures across the papers. They had ended their relationship of husband and wife.

Jaydeep and Sujata were married for eighteen years. Sujata had eloped with Jaydeep the day she had turned eighteen. Jaydeep and Sujata were neighbors. They had grown up together. Jaydeep was eight years senior to Sujata. Sujata had left her education and had broken all her ties with her family to be with Jaydeep. Jaydeep became successful. From an ordinary salesman, he progressed to be the owner of a factory. As he progressed in life, he started drifting away from Sujata.

Jaydeep was very busy in his life. Sujata had nothing to do. Her only solace was food. Shreya was their daughter. She was a grown up girl. She had become very independent. Shreya too had a lot of things to do.

Sujata would only sit at home and watch TV and eat something or the other. Jaydeep had maintained his physique. He would exercise and take care of himself.

Jaydeep was so fit that he did not look his age at all. Sujata had started looking elderly and she had lost all her charm.

Whenever she went out with Jaydeep for any social gatherings, she would hear people whisper. "What has Jaydeep found in this fatso"—sometimes it was fats, sometimes gunny bag and sometimes pumpkin. The superlatives changed every time. Jaydeep had tried to make Sujata understand in a hundred ways. He would constantly warn her about the dangers of obesity. Jaydeep had dragged her to a number of physicians. So many dieticians had chalked out diet plans for her. Sujata refused to follow these plans. She would follow the instructions for two days and the third day she would be back to her old ways.

Things worsened and there was no rapport between Jaydeep and Sujata. Both of them stopped having any normal conversation with each other. The arguments would sometimes be so loud that Shreya would plead to both of them to calm down. Shreya too was tired of the scene at home. Finally, one day Jaydeep gave his wife an ultimatum. He said he was tired of all this. He wanted to live peacefully. He told Sujata that he was filing a divorce on grounds of incompatibility. Sujata had never thought Jaydeep would take such a drastic step. The counselor at the family court failed to patch them up. Since Jaydeep had filed the divorce, he had to pay Sujata's alimony. Jaydeep had agreed to transfer their house in Sujata's name. Jaydeep was not bothered about the financial losses. He only wanted freedom from a dead marriage. Shreya opted to stay with her mother.

Sujata felt relieved when Jaydeep walked out. She felt it was better to live separately than fight like cats and dogs.

Sujata cleared the mess Jaydeep had created while leaving. Sujata made dinner for Shreya and herself. Shreya left for classes. She would be back by 7:30 pm. Sujata surfed the TV channels as usual. However, she couldn't bear to watch anything. Sujata decided to go for a walk. Sujata walked alone. Are physical appearances so important? Do all fat women get divorced? Just then, she saw a couple walk by. The wife was fat like her but her husband was holding her hands while they were walking. This is sheer bad luck. "This is destiny," she thought. I have to pay for all the trouble I caused my parents. Sujata's eyes swelled with tears when she remembered her baba. How sad her baba was when she eloped with Jaydeep. Her parents even shifted their residence. They couldn't bear the humiliation their daughter had caused.

Sujata looked at her mobile. "Oh God! Shreya would be back. I must go back. Poor thing, she would be worried. I have to live well for Shreya's sake. Poor girl! What will happen to her if anything goes wrong with me? Oh God! No! With my weight and the stress that I am going through, I am sure I will have a heart attack." Even the thought was so horrible.

Shreya had reached home before Sujata. "Where were you Ma? Your phone was also not reachable." Sujata said "Shreya I was feeling restless alone at home and so I went for a walk." Shreya hugged her mother tightly. "You are the best Ma! Both of them had a quiet dinner." Shreya felt asleep at once. Sujata didn't sleep a wink. She got up to see whether the main door was latched. She made sure the windows were closed. She heard the *Gurkha* beat his stick on the ground. Suddenly, Sujata felt very insecure. She had never felt insecure with Jaydeep around. "Now I understand the value of a man" she said.

Shreya got up early the next morning. Shreya missed her father. She put on a brave front "Ma can I bunk college today?" Sujata replied "If you are not feeling like going to college don't go, but don't bunk college for my sake. See Shreya, you have to work hard now. I want you to take up a respectable profession. Take up any course or degree of your choice but excel in whatever you do. I don't want you to land up in a sorry state like me. My baba would constantly tell me to concentrate on my studies. I didn't listen to him. I was blindfolded." Shreya asked "Ma do you regret marrying daddy?" Her mother responded "No Shreya, I don't regret anything in life. This was my destiny."

"I want you to be very smart. Shreya I don't want anyone to take advantage of you. Life is never complete without love, but it should happen at the right time. I will never stop you Shreya. The moment you like someone, please tell me. Shreya you are my only support now, I have to live only for you."

Both Shreya and Sujata hugged each other and started crying. "C'mon Shreya, today is the last time we are crying. Let's get back to work. You start getting ready for college. I will start making breakfast." "Why Ma? Wait for the maid to come." Sujata said "Shreya, I have sacked the maid. From today I will start doing all the work. This will keep me occupied." Shreya was surprised that her mother had changed so much overnight. Earlier, she would wait for the maid to make tea. She would not even get up to bring herself a glass of water.

Sujata finished all her household chores. She had nothing to do after that. She tried reading something but she couldn't concentrate. She turned to the TV. The usual *Saas Bahu* dramas were going on. She switched it off. She walked down. There was a deserted look everywhere. Everybody was busy. The society children had gone to school. The working women were in their respective offices. The men were engaged in their duties. Sujata felt as if she was the only person wandering aimlessly and without any work. Even the maids working in the society seemed to be in a hurry. Sujata walked for almost an hour. She was tired and sweating profusely and she decided to sit on the bench for some time.

When Sujata reached home, she looked at herself in the mirror. God! She hid her face in her hands. "How could I do this to myself?" Jaydeep's words kept on ringing in her ears. After Jaydeep had left, Sujata had realized the depth in his words. "What was wrong about Jaydeep's advice? I was stupid. How do I get rid of my fat now?" Sujata remembered that they had a lot of books on how to lose weight. She went through the books. The books were not even touched by her. She was surprised at the number of health magazines and health digests Jaydeep had subscribed for her.

Sujata was so engrossed in the books and magazines, she did not realize how the afternoon passed. She tried to summarize the tips and home remedies given in the books. She made a note of the things she wanted to do. Sujata realized that she had not had her lunch. "Oh no! Staying hungry is wrong. I need to eat, I need to eat smartly now. First of all I need to drink a lot of water. Let me make a nice note and stick it on the fridge." Sujata made two columns of Do and Don't.

Sujata remembered her friend Falguni. She had lost nearly 10 kg. Let me call her and ask her what she did. Sujata called Falguni. Falguni was very surprised to receive a call from Sujata. I thought you were happy in your own sweet world. Sujata told her about the divorce. Falguni was very sad. "Sujata I had been telling you this for so long. You just didn't understand. Anyways better late than never. From tomorrow, we work together. I am a fitness instructor now. I have a dietician in my gym who can help you." The same evening when Shreya came home, she was surprised to see her mother engrossed in reading books on health and weight loss.

"Shreya from tomorrow I will do as Falguni aunty tells me." Shreya said "Ma don't tell me what you are going to do. Just show me the results." Sujata said "Shreya just wait and see." Shreya said "OK. OK. Let's see."

Sujata went to a physician first. She wanted to be sure whether there was any medical cause for her obesity. The doctor advised her to undergo a series of investigations. "It is only your bad eating habits and lifestyle. Mrs Pandit you are lucky you are not having hypertension or diabetes.

With your weight you are inviting trouble." Falguni took her to a dietician. She chalked out a diet plan for Sujata. Sujata followed these plans. She walked in the mornings as well as in the evenings. Sujata lived on the fourth floor. She used the stairs instead of the lift.

Within a month, after dieting and exercising, Sujata lost about 4 to 5 kg. Sujata was in tears. "I put on weight so fast and now I am losing weight so slowly. At least you are losing weight, you are on a descending scale now." "Cheer up mumma!" Shreya tried to console her.

"Mumma today I am going out with daddy, so you will be alone in the evening." Sujata felt very bad. Jaydeep had not bothered to speak to her on the phone or even bothered to see how she was since he had left.

Sujata didn't say anything to Shreya. Her only aim was to look like her old self. "I know I won't be the same, but at least I can try."

Sujata joined a gym. The gym instructor was very pleased with her enthusiasm. "Madam if you work with the same enthusiasm the results will start showing. You will be the face of our gym." Sujata was taken aback with the instructor's words. She was the first person to enter the gym every morning and she let out all her frustrations and anger in the workouts. Within six months, Sujata lost a lot of weight. Sujata gained a lot of confidence. Shreya too was surprised to see the metamorphosis in her mother.

Sujata became a fitness freak. Her world revolved only around diet and exercise. All the neighbors, everybody who knew Sujata before, were very surprised to see her now. "Does she look like a mother of a seventeen year old?" they wondered.

Sujata became very popular. The gym where she went put her posters up. Sujata then and Sujata now. Sujata was very pleased with herself. Sujata joined the gym as an instructor.

Whenever she was free, Sujata browsed the Internet to see what was happening in the world of fitness in different parts of the world. Sujata became a very well read person and she knew everything about diet and fitness. More and more women joined the same gym. She did a course in aerobics and yoga as well.

The owner of the gym was very happy with Sujata's performance. Sujata had never ever imagined that one day she would be helping people to lose weight and lead a healthy lifestyle.

Jaydeep was unaware of Sujata's developments. Once when he happened to drop Shreya he bumped into Sujata. Jaydeep couldn't believe his eyes. "Is this Sujata?" he thought. "Sujata how are you?"

Sujata said she was fine and walked away. She didn't even bother to call him in the house. She had an appointment with a very important client who was to join the gym.

Modern Day Princess

Pushpa returned home after a long tiring day. Her daughter Sayogita opened the door for her. Pushpa's face lit up the moment she saw her. "Sayyu, my Sayyu is going to look gorgeous" she said to herself. "Why are you late today mummy?" Pushpa said "I had to finish the drafting for tomorrow's case for Mr Naik." Pushpa was Mr Shripad Naik's personal secretary. Mr Naik was one of Pune's leading lawyers. Pushpa was his right hand. She was working with him for almost twenty years now.

Sayyu made a cup of tea and brought it for Pushpa. Instead of being pleased with Sayyu's gesture, she reprimanded Sayyu. "Don't waste your time doing mediocre things Sayogita. You are not meant for these jobs. I work hard only for you Sayyu. I don't want you to go through what I have gone through. I want you to excel in academics. I want you to do well in life. It's my dream, that you have a fleet of servants and secretaries at your beck and call." Sayyu went quietly to her study table. Pushpa went to the kitchen to make dinner for them.

Pushpa thought "Mohan would be back from work. He always wanted to have an early dinner." Mohan worked as a supervisor in an automobile company. Mohan was a very satisfied person. He was happy with whatever he earned. He had a laid back attitude. In fact, he was very happy of his achievements in life. He aIways said that he had never dreamt that he would be a supervisor. He was very satisfied that he was supervising two hundred to three hundred workers.

Mohan earned enough for three of them to lead a comfortable life.

Pushpa was just the opposite. She was very ambitious, but life had not given her the right opportunities.

Her only aim in life was to make her daughter Sayyogita an I.A.S. officer.

Pushpa's entire salary was spent on Sayyogita's education. Sayogita went to the best school in Pune. Sayyogita went for extra coaching classes in languages and she learnt music.

Pushpa's entire life revolved around Sayyogita's studies and classes.

Sayyogita was good at studies. She was among the top three students in her class. Sayyogita was very scared of her mother. She had very few friends. Pushpa had brainwashed Sayyogita in such a way that she too believed that her only aim in life was to be an I.A.S. officer.

At times, Pushpa also felt that she was being too hard on Sayyogita. When she had such thoughts in her mind, she pulled herself and said that if she wanted Sayyogita to succeed she had to be strict with her. Mohan was a silent spectator to all the events happening around him.

Sayyogita completed her graduation successfully. Pushpa and Sayyogita went for a talk conducted by the coaching class for I.A.S exams.

Pushpa was taken aback when she heard that boys and girls usually attended classes while doing their undergraduation.

Pushpa was surprised to hear the number of people who aspired to be in the administrative services.

Pushpa got Sayyogita enrolled in the most famous coaching classes.

Pushpa said "Sayyogita, don't bother about anything. Remember our aim is to crack the UPSC examinations."

Pushpa was worried for thc first time. She felt her confidence wane after attending the induction program. She murmured "God! I was carried away by the glamor of the post. I never thought how difficult it is to crack these competitive exams." Mohan warned Pushpa several times. He did not want Pushpa to be strict with their daughter. "She is our only daughter. Just see that she doesn't break down with the stress." Whenever Mohan talked about this, Pushpa asked him to keep quiet. He said "I really can't understand how to deal with you Pushpa. How can you be so strict with your own child?"

Sayyogita attended the coaching classes for long hours. At other times, she read books. She had to read books on English language, history, geography, science and general knowledge. Every week, Sayyogita appeared for mock tests.

Sayyogita's day began by reading all the newspapers. She had to know everything that was happening around her.

Mohan said "I wonder how you will remember so many things." Whenever Mohan said this, Pushpa said "The human brain is a computer. The brain can store any amount of knowledge." Sayyogita's room was cramped with books. In fact, every nook and cranny was occupied by books. Sayyogita was cramped up on her study table.

Sayyogita studied for twelve to thirteen hours every day.

Pushpa left no stone unturned for Sayyo's success. She went every day to Sarasbaug Ganapati. Sayyogita was obsessed with her studies. Pushpa was obsessed with her puja's and fasts for Sayyo.

Sayyogita saw from where all people came to attend classes to prepare for the UPSC exams. Sayyogita's confidence was shaken. Till now, she believed that she was the best. When she saw the other boys and girls in her classes, she did not feel the same.

She thought "I have to crack the exams in the first attempt." Everyone discussed only one thing. How difficult it was to crack the Administrative Service examinations.

Sayyo's father was very scared of the whole scenario. He spent sleepless nights when he noticed Sayyo's plight. "She's overburdened" he said. He often said this to Pushpa. "You are fulfilling your personal desires and dreams through her. You have made her a puppet."

Once, Sayyu was very dejected after attending the classes. She had been unable to solve her paper at the mock test. Instead of consoling her and encouraging her Pushpa shouted at her. "I am a fool to expect anything from you, you can't crack a mock test and I have dreams to see you crack the UPSC exams." Mohan heard their conversation and intervened "Enough is enough! Sayyu will not attend any classes. She will not appear for any examinations. I will find a job for her and find a nice boy and get her married."

Pushpa had not expected Mohan to shout at her. She behaved very wisely. She hugged Sayyu tightly and said "See dear, I know what your father means. He will do exactly as he wants. This is what I was afraid of."

Poor Sayyu was caught between her parent's egos. She decided that it was better to not think about the mock test.

Next morning, Sayyu got up as usual at 3 am. She had to make up for the evening she had lost yesterday. Sayyu assured her father that she would not succumb to any pressure. She planned her studies systematically. She thought about the best way to cover history, geography and civics. She read school textbooks. She felt it was the easiest way to cover all the three subjects.

Her languages were very strong. So she was not scared of English language. She wrote essays and got them corrected from different English professors.

Once she wrote an easy on "What changes should be brought in the Indian judicial system?" Pushpa showed Sayyu's essay to Mr Shripad Naik. Mr Naik was very impressed with Sayyu's essay. This boosted her confidence.

Sayyu appeared for the prelims in order to qualify for the mains. All Sayyu's efforts brought her success. She scored well in the prelims and qualified for the mains.

Sayyu prepared for the mains. Her mentors at the coaching institute were very pleased and happy with Sayyogita Patankar's performance.

There were students who took two to three attempts to qualify for the mains.

Sayyu had three to four months in hand to study for the mains. Sayyu was very charged now. She ate, slept and dreamt only about what could be asked for the mains.

Pushpa took leave for three months. She felt she had to be there to look after Sayyu and boost her confidence.

Pushpa visited an astrologer to ask if Sayyu's stars would favor her during her mains.

The astrologer said "Sayyu is born to hold a lucrative position." Pushpa's joys knew no bounds when she heard this.

Pushpa shared this with Mohan. "God always helps those who put in so much of efforts." Even Pushpa and Mohan had started reading competition success review and all the possible newspapers. They also tried to update Sayyu with the latest news in the world. Pushpa always thought "What use is this knowledge of Art and Modern Architecture?" How was it going to help these

I.A.S. officers? Why are they so burdened with so many subjects? They even had to appear for examination in science as well.

Pushpa was stressed when she thought about Sayyu and her examinations. Finally, the day for the exams arrived. Sayyu and Pushpa traveled to Navi Mumbai for the exams.

Sayyu had to write a two-hour examination. Pushpa sat outside the exam center and read the "Guru Charitra."

Sayyu cleared the mains. Now Sayyu and Pushpa had to travel to Delhi for the Interview. It was the first time both of them were traveling outside the state.

Pushpa was scared but she put on a brave front. Sayyu gained super confidence on the day of her interview. She asked her mother to remain cool.

Sayyu's confidence and perseverance made her sail safely through the interview.

Sayyu and Pushpa returned to Pune. Pushpa was not sure about Sayyu's success. Pushpa got up in the middle of the night. She was sweating profusely. Every day seemed to pass at a snail's pace.

Sayyu was busy interacting with her friends. This was something that she had not done for ages. Her friend Medha's wedding got fixed. Sayyu was busy with Medha in doing all the preparations for the wedding.

One day, when Mohan was alone at home their landline started ringing and someone at the other end was calling from Times Now, the famous TV channel asking for Sayyogita Patankar. "*Woh ghar par nahi hai*" said Mohan. The person said that she had scored the ninety-seventh rank in the UPSC exams. Mohan felt as though the world had suddenly taken a big spin. His hands trembled. His voice cracked.

"My Sayyu, my Sayyu," that's all he said. He called Pushpa and Sayyu to convey the good news. "Don't play jokes" said Sayyu. It was a dream come true. Congratulatory calls kept pouring in. Journalists from all newspapers came to click her pictures. Reporters from all TV channels and newspapers came to interview Sayyu. It was after a very long time that a girl from Pune had scored such a high rank at UPSC exams.

The journalists took Mohan and Pushpa's interviews as well. Sayyu had become a celebrity now. Relatives and friends who had distanced themselves from the Patankar's suddenly came to congratulate them.

Now Sayyu had to go to Mussoorie for training at the Lal Bahadur Shastri National Academy of Administration (LBSNAA). Pushpa was very sad as it was the first time she would stay away from her.

Mohan and Pushpa went all the way to Mussoorie to leave Sayyu.

Sayyu began a new chapter in her life. She made a lot of friends here at LBSNAA. Those days were really magical, so they just flew away. She had to do Bharat Darshan with her fellow colleagues. Sayyu traveled extensively across India. Sayyu dined in exclusive restaurants. She also had community lunches in Gurudwaras. Now she really understood why the term "Incredible India" was formed. Sayyu was invited for dinner at the Rashtrapati Bhavan as well. Sayyu clicked pictures with the President. The President also spoke to her personally. The eighteen months training at LBSNAA just flew away.

Sayogita Patankar opted for Maharashtra Cadre. She got posted as Asst. Collector of Kolhapur.

Sayyogita convinced Mohan to take voluntary retirement. Pappa, I want you to only relax and enjoy now. Mr Naik also said that Pushpa should go with her daughter to Kolhapur.

Mr Naik threw a grand party in Sayyogita's honor. Even Mr Shripad Naik was choked up when he spoke of Sayyogita's achievements. He mentioned how Sayyu quietly studied in his office while her mother typed his citations.

The Patankars moved into the new bungalow that was allotted to them. Sayyu had a car and a driver. She had a cook at home. Sayyogita was very happy to join work. Sayyogita worked very hard for maintaining the law and order in her district. She realized that the farmers in her district were not using modern methods of agriculture as they did not have funds to do so. She made loans available easily for them from the co-operative banks. The Collector was very pleased with Sayyogita's work. At other places, there were disputes because of lack of co-operation among the office bearers. Sayyogita's temperament was such that she worked in harmony with everyone. Sayyogita also implemented programs for giving the women financial independence. She encouraged woman to set up small-scale businesses. She encouraged women to take up textile making. She revived the looms in Ichalkaranji. Sayyogita worked from six in the morning to midnight.

Pushpa and Mohan felt that it was high time that she should settle in life. Pushpa started looking out for prospective bride grooms. No proposal seemed to be right. Everybody had some hidden agenda in marrying Sayyogita.

Pushpa even registered her name in several matrimonial agencies. Mohan worried day and night about Sayyogita's marriage. This affected Mohan's health. The stress made Mohan suffer from hypertension and diabetes.

Pushpa asked several astrologers when Sayyogita would get married. Pushpa even performed several "Pujas" and "Shantis" so that Sayyogita would get married.

Nothing seemed to work. "This is the price we have to pay for her success."

Sayyogita was so engrossed in her work that she didn't have time to think about anything.

Sayyogita had become a workaholic. All her frustrations were channelized into energy to work.

Sayyogita loved children. Now even she started regretting that she had not got married.

Sayyogita had a strong maternal instinct. She had decided to adopt a girl child.

One morning, she made this announcement to her parents. “Pappa and mumma, I have decided to adopt a girl from the orphanage. I will get her home once all the legal formalities are completed.”

Pushpa and Mohan were shocked to hear this. They said in unison “This will ruin your chances of getting married Sayyu.”

Sayyu was adamant. “Mumma please allow me to take at least one decision in my life. Another thing, I don’t want any of your interference in my daughter’s upbringing. I want my girl to grow in such a way that she has the freedom to live life at her terms and conditions.” Pushpa was flabbergasted. This was something which she never expected.